Original 1951 Dedication

for
HERTHA DEPPER

a fine artist and a lovely friend

Behold Your Queen!

A Story of Esther

By
Gladys Malvern

Edited by
Susan Houston

Special Edition Books

Behold Your Queen! A Story of Esther
By Gladys Malvern
Edited by Susan Houston, Shawn Conners

First Printing – February 2011

Published by
Special Edition Books
El Paso, Texas USA

ISBN10: 1-934255-84-X
ISBN13: 978-1-934255-84-1

Printed in the United States of America

Foreword

The books we read as children are often the most lasting. They are the ones we mentally refer back to as adults, when we find something new that we really like. These books aren't necessarily literary classics… in fact, they are more likely not; but the ideas and storylines linger long past childhood. I was passionately fond of historical and biblical fiction from childhood on, and *Behold Your Queen!* covered both. Queen Esther's story from the Old Testament is a prime example of the stories, myths and fairy tales we tell our children to teach them basic concepts of virtue, heroism, courage and love.

Behold Your Queen! is a "hidden princess story," which no woman can resist; the idea that within each of us is a person of such innate strength and beauty that regardless of our birth, we are worthy of the honor of being a queen and being loved by a king. I wanted to be like Esther--Malvern's description of how her Uncle Mordecai "had taught her to sit quietly, often for an hour at a time," made me want to learn that sort of stillness. She had endless patience, self-control, unselfishness and many other qualities of character that I wanted to have too.

About Gladys Malvern

Gladys Malvern wrote almost 4 dozen books in her prolific career as a writer of Young Adult fiction and biography. She was born in New Jersey on July 17, 1897, though her roots were in Virginia and her ancestors include such historic American names as Lee, Rolfe, Randolph, and Custis. Her mother, Cora Malvern, worked as a wardrobe mistress for theater companies, and Gladys and her younger sister Corinne worked as child actresses in plays, vaudeville, and operas. By 1910 the two sisters were working regularly in traveling vaudeville productions, as well as in the growing New York movie industry.

By 1930 Gladys Malvern was a sales manager for a department store; Corinne, and their mother were living together in Los Angeles. The Malvern family moved to New York sometime between 1934 and 1936, and Gladys settled down to writing, sharing a studio with her sister Corinne overlooking the Hudson River. Corinne illustrated most of Gladys' books until her death in 1956. Gladys wrote in a variety of formats, including short stories, advertising copy and radio scripts, but was happiest when writing for young adults.

Susan Houston
February, 2011

Contents

1: Hadassah

HADASSAH picked up the bundle containing a silk scarf she was making for Sarah, and with her free hand put on a veil. Though no respectable Hebrew maiden was ever seen in public without a veil, few wore one which completely hid the face and half of the body. Most of them wore veils which only covered their heads to the eyebrows and hung to the shoulders in the back. But Uncle Mordecai insisted that Hadassah wear the full veil, and to disobey him was unthinkable. Still, the sun was brighter than usual, the air was heavy with the heat, and she grumbled as she put on the veil.

I shall smother in this, she thought.

Only yesterday she had tried to convince her uncle that it was no longer stylish to look like a mummy on the street.

"But," she insisted, "the long veil is outmoded!"

He had looked at her calmly and answered in his quiet way.

"Still, I wish you to wear it."

He could not tell her that she was more beautiful than other girls, that hers was the kind of face—so lovely in its coloring, so flawless in skin texture, so appealing in the delicacy of its modeling—that men would stare after her on the street, and that some—especially the Amalekites, who were notoriously objectionable where feminine pulchritude was concerned—would cause embarrassment for her.

On the way out now, Hadassah stopped long enough to tell the old woman the one female servant of the house where she was going and when she would return, and then hurried into the sun-baked street.

The Hebrew population of Babylon lived in its own quarter on the left bank of the river, a city within a city. Here its residents could purchase everything needed—oils, fabrics, food, perfumes, ointments, sandals, candles and house furnishings; consequently it was never necessary to venture into Babylon itself. The Hebrew quarter was not so populous now as it had been when Hadassah was little, because from year to year families who could afford the journey were returning to the Holy Land.

Over forty-two thousand had already left, mostly members of the tribe of Judah and of her own tribe, Benjamin. But Mordecai loved Babylon, and though he almost beggared himself sending money to Jerusalem to help in rebuilding the temple, he had no desire to make the difficult nine-hundred mile journey. Over a hundred pounds of gold and five hundred pounds of silver he had contributed so far.

Mordecai, Hadassah had long ago discovered, was different from other people. His neighbors, for instance, were aghast when one day he had taken his niece across the bridge into the pagan city of Babylon. All the other girls were curious about it, and when she returned they begged Hadassah to tell them what it was like.

"I know," Mordecai explained, "that it is natural that Babylon should hold a certain lure for you. I will take you there myself and show you the sights, and when you have seen it, you will be content to remain in your own quarter where you belong."

It had been an exciting day. The splendid city, its wide streets teeming with people from all over the world, thrilled and impressed her. Here were great astronomical laboratories. Here were men grinding upon a wheel the crystal lenses to be used in the study of the stars. And the temples! Oh, the gorgeous temples to so many strange gods!

Brilliant and luxurious as Babylon was, Hadassah had been glad to return to her own quarter where she felt at home. The quarter was serene, even austere, and compared to that towering city across the river, it seemed so humble.

Here and there a blossoming tree, a vivid vine, showed bravely against the low brick houses. In the small gardens one glimpsed fig and orange trees, pampered, treasured.

Turning up a side street now, Hadassah felt the friendliness of this tiny, familiar world of hers. She was fourteen and filled with romantic dreams. Fourteen. Seemingly, for a long, long time she had been waiting to be fourteen. At fourteen a girl had reached the age when her father or guardian could arrange a marriage for her.

It was natural that Hadassah should be thinking of marriage today, for Sarah had been betrothed only a week before, and from now on her friends would meet in the Women's Court of her house to sew and make donations to her huge carved chest of cedarwood which contained her mounting pile of bridal garments and linens.

Hadassah was on the threshold of her friend's house now.

In response to her knock, a servant opened the door. Recognizing Hadassah, he nodded toward the rear where the women's quarters were. Hadassah knew the way.

It led through a narrow hall into a walled courtyard, shaded by awnings. Here were chairs, benches and several small tables. On the tables were pottery dishes containing figs, pomegranates, dates and small cakes at which the girls nibbled from time to time.

At sight of Hadassah several young voices rose in greeting.

Sarah, looking dignified and important because she was betrothed, came forward politely.

"Hadassah! *Baruch habavah*! Welcome!" They kissed.

There were five girls, whose ages ranged from fourteen to sixteen. Several of them were already engaged, but being well brought up, they acted as though they were not in the least curious about marriage. So, as they worked, they discussed other matters.

Their prime topic was the king and queen. King Ahasuerus was a glamorous, young figure. Queen Vashti was renowned as the most beautiful woman in the world. She set the fashions, not only in clothes but in manners.

"They say," said Sarah, biting a thread with her crooked teeth, "that the queen prefers yellow this season. What a pity! I look hideous in yellow, but I shall have to have yellow robes." She shrugged. "Who wants to be out of fashion?"

"I wonder how it would feel to be a queen?" asked Hadassah in her beautifully modulated voice.

Her companions looked at her curiously, for only she among them could boast of having royal blood. She was a direct descendant of King Saul. Though the house she lived in was modest and she was far from being the richest girl in the community, Hadassah was royalty.

And, they had to admit, she looked it. She was only slightly above medium height, but she gave the impression of being taller because of her long legs, her long, slender neck, and the proud, spirited way she had of holding her head.

"Has anyone asked for you yet?" asked Sarah after a slight pause.

"I think not," replied the girl candidly. "At any rate, my uncle has told me nothing about it."

"Perhaps," put in Rebecca, "he thinks no one is good enough for you."

The others waited a trifle anxiously, expecting her to reply angrily at this rudeness, but she only shrugged in a good-natured way and continued her sewing. "I know not the thoughts of my uncle, but—I'm not sure that I want to marry."

There were shocked gasps. "Not want to marry!" exclaimed Sarah. "Why, what else is there for a woman?"

"Besides, it is a sin not to wed," added Leah righteously. "To have an unmarried daughter would be a disgrace to your tribe."

"I know," Hadassah admitted. "But I think it would be unbearably sad to leave my uncle. It is different with the rest of you. Your parents have large families, but Uncle Mordecai has only me."

Hadassah looked up from her sewing, gazing thoughtfully at Rebecca and Sarah and some of the others who were betrothed. Certainly, she was not so scrawny as Rebecca. Sarah had bad teeth, and Leah had pimples. She longed to ask Mordecai, "Has no one asked for me in marriage to his son?" But this would not be proper. She must pretend that she had no interest in the matter. But someday—any day now—he would surely come to her and say, his face grave and his voice serene, "I have decided upon so and so, son of so and so, for you."

And she would bow her head and reply respectfully, "Let it be as my uncle wills."

Somewhat concernedly, she wondered how Mordecai would feel about it. Would he be glad when that time came? Would he say to himself, "She is no longer my responsibility?" Between herself and this scholarly, undemonstrative man there had always been a deep affection. Hadassah had always been proud of her uncle, who was the most important person in their district.

At that very moment, on the other side of the quarter, Mordecai's friend, Isaac ben Ezra, had come to him at the table on the corner where Mordecai sat in his long robe with a reed pen behind his ear as the symbol of his profession, and the carefully wound turban of a scribe on his head.

“So, Isaac!" began Mordecai heartily. "And is it a letter you want me to write to your brother in Jerusalem?"

"No, Mordecai. It is another matter. Your niece has passed her fourteenth birthday."

Mordecai nodded, leaning back in his chair. "As my friend has said."

"My son was eighteen yesterday. He is of age for marriage. The Commandment is that man shall not live alone."

Mordecai's voice was cold. "You are asking me for Hadassah?"

"I am."

"She is too young."

"Too young? Fourteen? It is the proper age for espousal."

"But Hadassah seems such a child. I prefer to wait before betrothing her."

Isaac glared. "There is not a youth in Babylon who can give her more. Perhaps you think because she has a king for an ancestor that my son is not good enough."

"I have nothing against your son. He is an estimable young man, but I intend to wait until Hadassah is sixteen before accepting any offers for her."

Mordecai was not surprised when his friend left huffily.

Alone at his table he toyed with the pieces of papyrus and the clay tablets before him.

He was a handsome man of thirty-seven. His hair was black, crisp, abundant. His beard was curled in the Persian manner and lustrous with sweetly scented oil. His eyes were bright and kindly, the eyes of a man who had taught himself to take in much at a single glance. They were thoughtful eyes now, as memory drew him back through the years.

His grandfather, Shimei, son of Kish, with his large family, had been taken captive when Jerusalem had fallen to the overwhelming forces of Nebuchaddnezzar, who was the king of Babylon. Every able-bodied resident of Jerusalem had been brought to Babylon in shackles. All the mighty in the land, including Jehoiachin, the Hebrew king, the king's mother, his wives, his officers, the crown prince, seven thousand craftsmen, one thousand smiths, all the princes—over ten thousand people in chains, burdened with loot, marched the nine hundred miles over hills and desert, miserable, beaten, disgraced.

Many had been unable to endure the hardships of the brutal journey. Among those who had perished on the way had been Mordecai's grandfather, the once powerful Shimei, and every member of his family except Mordecai's father, Jair.

A lad of less than ten years, Jair had come to Babylon a prisoner. At first, he had seen his people persecuted and looked down upon by the haughty, idol-worshipping Babylonians. As the years passed, however, the Israelites had proved so useful to Nebuchaddnezzar that, while still technically slaves and forbidden to migrate to other cities, they had been given positions of trust.

Gradually they had been permitted to own houses, open their own businesses and establish themselves in their own quarter. In time they came to feel at home in this new country. So Jair, of the tribe of Benjamin, son of Shimei, son of Kish, had grown to manhood in Babylon. Here he married. All of Jair's offspring had died of a plague except Mordecai and his sister, Abibhail, who was four years Mordecai's junior.

The two had been warmly attached, and Mordecai had been happy when Abibhail became betrothed to their cousin, Solomon ben Joses. After five years of marriage, when Abibhail had given birth to Hadassah, Mordecai had been both uncle and cousin to the child.

In this country, where the Israelites were surrounded and governed by people not of their religion, it had become the custom to give each girl-baby two names—one, the Hebrew name by which she was known among her own kind; the other, the Babylonian name to be used only when she was introduced to outsiders. So Abibhail's daughter had been given the Hebrew name of Hadassah, which meant "myrtle" or "bride," and also the name then popular in Babylon, Esther, which had been derived from the name of a goddess—Ishtar, and meant "star."

When Hadassah was a year old her father had been killed in an altercation with an Amalekite. He had left the house smiling, walking quickly, humming a song. He had been brought back a lifeless, blood-soaked hulk.

To seek to punish the offender would have availed the Hebrews nothing. When such things happened, they quietly buried their dead, and the ancient hatred against their old enemies, the Amalekites, was intensified.

Abibhail's grief had been so intense that she lost all interest in life, even in her child. Six months later she caught a fever and died. So Mordecai ben Jair, a youth of twenty-three, had taken into his house this tiny orphan, a year and a half old.

There was nothing else he could do. He alone was responsible for the child, since she had no other living relative. From the first this child had filled his life. He loved holding her in his arms and she would cling to him with fierce, tight little hands. He determined then to mould her into his ideal of womanhood. Here was a life given to him to form, much as a sculptor moulded clay .

He had seen to it that she was well educated. Himself a brilliant scholar, he was her only teacher. Though it was not considered necessary for a woman to read, he taught her to read and to cipher. He taught her the history of her own people as well as the histories of Persia and Babylonia. Too, he taught her the poetry of the Israelites, the psalms, of which there were over a hundred. He watched her manners. He taught her to hold herself proudly and to carry herself with a queenly grace.

He was watchful of her diction. He saw to it that her speaking voice was low and smooth. He had her taught singing and playing the dulcimer. He instilled in her a flawless taste in clothes. He even taught her to use her hands in such a way that every gesture was eloquent and beautiful. He insisted that she brush and anoint her hair and keep it lustrous, clean and sweet smelling. In addition she was versed in the usual things such as housekeeping, cooking, candlemaking, spinning, weaving and embroidering.

And now he could look at her and say, "I have done well. I have nothing more to teach her." And now that she was a perfect specimen of womanhood, now it was time for her to leave his house! Well, he must face this, since it was inevitable, but he was determined to postpone it.

The sun was setting when Mordecai's manservant came and gathered up the papers and the small table, and followed him through the streets to his home. It was not an ornate house, but its furnishings were comfortable and tasteful. Though Hadassah managed with only one female servant, everything ran smoothly and in perfect order.

As he entered he found Hadassah and the old woman preparing supper. The girl looked up at him and smiled fondly, thinking how handsome he was—tall, well built and strong. Her face slightly flushed from the heat of the oven, Hadassah brought him clean sandals.

"Today," she said as she stooped to put them on her uncle's feet, "I went to Sarah's."

"So?"

"As my uncle knows, she is betrothed. So are Leah and Rebecca."

"That is natural. That is good. Someday we will have a betrothal in this house. Do you wish for it, child?"

"Let it be in accord with my uncle's will," she answered simply. "But I am happy here. I think I could be no happier anywhere, not even in the king's palace."

He patted her shoulder affectionately. "In the palace of the king, my child, there is too much of everything. We are blessed as we are. We have enough to eat, enough to wear, enough to buy books, enough to give to charity, enough to contribute to the building of the temple in Jerusalem. What more could we ask?"

"Dinner is ready," announced the old woman.

As she spoke, there came the sound of trumpets. She grumbled as she moved the food away from the heat, for now the meal would have to wait.

With their servants, Mordecai and his niece hastened out of the house moving toward the Place of Assembly. They were in the midst of a crowd, everyone hurrying in the same direction. Whole families with their servants moved quickly, eager to return to their meal and equally eager to hear what would be announced. Would it be good or bad?

When an official announcement was to be made, the trumpeters proceeded to the various sections of the metropolis and summoned the people by blowing upon their instruments. In the Places of Assembly the people stood quietly while a member of the government pompously mounted a high marble block and proclaimed the news.

He was walking up the stairs to the top of it now, a garland on his head and his hairy arms covered with bracelets.

"His Majesty, Ahasuerus the mighty, king of the Medes and Persians and all the country from India to Ethiopia sends his greeting to his loyal subjects. He proclaims a celebration on the anniversary of the third year of his reign, a holiday of one week is decreed for all people, while, for one hundred and eighty-seven days, his noble Majesty entertains his friends, as well as ambassadors from foreign countries and lords and governors of his one hundred and twenty-seven satrapies, at the palace in Shushan. He desires that this time of festival be shared by all his kingdom."

Shouts went up in praise of the decree. Oh, they thought, as they turned homeward again, he is good, this brave young king of ours!

Behind her thick veil Hadassah's eyes were bright. It seemed to Mordecai that presently she would break into a gay skip-and-run as children do when their hearts are full of joy.

"We have a wonderful king," she cried gleefully. "Oh, I would like to see him!"

"But you have seen statues of him." Mordecai took a coin from the pouch at his belt. "Here, stamped on this metal you can see his profile."

"I mean I would like to see him face to face. And yet, I wonder, if he is so good, why does he permit the Amalekites to do such hateful things?"

"He cannot know everything that goes on."

"Still, he cannot be ignorant of those detestable Amalekites." Like every other Hebrew, Hadassah had been trained to fear, distrust and loathe the Amalekites. It was an old, old feud, dating back to the days before Saul.

"Many people considered Nebuchaddnezzar a good king." said Mordecai quietly, "yet under his rule Zedekiah had his eyes put out after watching the Babylonians kill his entire family. The king of Babylon had the temple at Jerusalem burnt to the ground. The whole city was laid waste, and the king of Babylon himself led the blinded king of the Hebrews and the thousands of heartbroken prisoners to this place. So, you see, even the best of kings—"

Hadassah was a child of the present. At the moment she was not interested in the past and the cruelties of a now dead ruler. Three years ago when the new king came into power after the assassination of his father, she had been eleven years old. To her, from the first, Ahasuerus had been a hero. She looked upon him as even more than king. Her childish imagination had exalted him to a being above human frailty, and she could not understand why, under the rulership of this flawless young hero, the power of the Amalekites had steadily increased.

Hadassah recalled now that there was a saying, "As in the king's house, so is it in the kingdom." If the king had a festival, the whole empire feasted. If the queen wore yellow, every woman bought yellow. If the king honored an Amalekite, the Amalekites were honored everywhere. And Haman, the prime minister, was an Amalekite.

So it was that in any case at law involving an Amalekite and a Hebrew, verdict was invariably given in favor of the former. Knowing this the Hebrews avoided their enemies as much as possible. Passing an Amalekite on the street, they gave him wide room, for an Amalekite could jostle a Hebrew, run him down with a horse, cheat him, even beat him physically and the Hebrew had no redress.

And yet—the king was just. How then were these things possible?

Mordecai spoke in his wise, calm way. "When we look back over the history of the world, we see that sometimes evil rules—but God does not permit it to endure. A day comes when it is unveiled and overthrown. So, child, have faith that in His own time, God will cause someone to be his instrument to rid our country of this intolerable injustice!"

2: "As in the King's House . . . "

THE YOUNG king walked with Prime Minister Haman, his bodyguard and his retinue of chamberlains through room after room of the palace, making the final inspection before the arrival of his guests. The jewels, the plate, the trophies old and new, were all on display. Here were pictures, statues, statuettes, rugs, countless objects of art, each exhibited in perfect settings, the best in Persia and that meant the best in the world.

Next he inspected the gardens, where the choicest plants and trees had been grouped in consummate artistry, their colors richly blending, their sizes measured, so that every bloom and bush lent its loveliness to one vast panorama of perfect symmetry.

This was no ordinary occasion. Aristocrats and politicians were coming from every part of the world. It was well that they should view for themselves the power, the grandeur, the unlimited wealth of Persia.

Ahasuerus wanted peace. The way to maintain peace was to impress all rulers with his affluence and his might. So he was giving this feast, putting on this stupendous show, not—as some people were whispering—because of personal vanity, but because of a recent council which he had held to consider the pros and cons of an invasion of Greece. The question was: Was Greece even now marshalling her forces to invade Persia, or should Persia invade Greece?

Ahasuerus, whose name meant "mighty" or "lion-hearted," or "the lion-king," had been reared as a warrior. His father's reign had been one long interval of war. One country after another had been conquered, with the exception of Greece. Greece remained—a challenge and a threat. As crown prince, even before he was ten, Ahasuerus had been in the midst of war, accompanying his father on every campaign. He had fought like a hero. But now he was determined to preserve peace if possible.

So, he had decided upon this celebration, decided to invite, not only the princes and governors of his own conquered countries, but representatives and potentates of other countries, reasoning that if they saw for themselves the wealth and military power of Persia, they would report to their own people the futility of making an attack upon her. They must know that he had absolute control over his people. They must also know that boundless though his resources were, he desired peace.

He was a tall young man, and in appearance every inch a king. Dark in the manner of Persians, with heavily lidded eyes, a thin, straight nose, and a lean bearded face. It was a strong face with a mouth which, though full, was firm. His body was lithe as a panther's, disciplined, regal. Those who knew him, watched his eyes in order to gauge his mood. Those eyes had a way of changing with magical swiftness. At times they were the eyes of a boy, glowing with humor, mischief, excitement; at times they were the dreamy eyes of a poet; but in a second they could glitter with fury, and at times they were the meditative eyes of a priest; but usually, they were hard, wise, suspicious, world-weary, intensely serious and probing.

Three years of kingship had made that handsome face appear older than it should have been at twenty-one, but occasionally he broke into a warm smile or a hearty laugh, and then the tenseness, the strain fell away, and he seemed only a boy, trustful, humorous, appealing.

The king and his party came now to a large tent of purple linen, supported by pillars of pure gold and silver. It was sufficiently commodious to seat tens of thousands. Already on the tables were hundreds of solid gold cups, each different, and each encrusted with precious stones. Here his guests would lunch and partake of refreshments throughout the day, but the final banquet for each group would take place in the state banquet room.

Leaving the tent, the party strolled through the gardens. The face of the young king became lovable and boyish as he paused before an enormous bed of white and crimson peonies. The seeds had been brought from a distant Mongol country and were new to Persia. With the tenderness of a woman his strong hands touched one of the fully opened flowers, caressing it as though it were a living thing. But he swiftly reminded himself that he could not linger there gazing in rapturous appreciation at flowers. He must go on to other, more pressing matters.

This youth was absolute master of millions, He was no weakling. As crown prince he had never been pampered. His life had not been one of softness because of his exalted position.

He had been given an excellent scholastic education, his studies beginning at five and continuing for fifteen years. Never was he permitted to sleep after dawn. Upon arising he was put through relentless exercises including running and the handling of weapons. None of his soldiers could handle the big bows more expertly than he.

At seven his training in horsemanship had begun. Even at that age he had been forced to endure brutal extremes of heat and cold. At twelve he had been compelled to make long marches, to sleep in the open, to hunt lions, and live on five meals a week. At fourteen he had been sent for months into the hills alone. Here, unaided, he had had to fight whatever wild beasts he had encountered and subsist on whatever wild berries and game he could find. In addition he had been instructed in law, morals, diplomacy and religion. All of this had been for the purpose of fitting him to occupy the lofty position to which, three years ago, he had been so suddenly called.

"His Majesty is satisfied?" asked Haman in that smooth, ingratiating voice of his.

The king turned to him, his eyes filled with affection. "Quite—father."

To call Haman "father" was the greatest compliment he could pay. Haman was more than twice his age. Only four years ago he had arrived in Shushan from Macedonia, poor and unknown. Since then he had been promoted and enriched, and as one promotion speedily followed another, his self-confidence had increased.

Those close to the throne, those who felt a sincere affection for the young king, often wondered why a man like Haman could have attained such dominion over the young monarch.

They would have understood this, could they had looked into the mind of the boy-ruler at the time of his father's tragic death.

True, Ahasuerus had been trained to be a king, but he had not dreamed that the gigantic responsibility would fall upon him so suddenly—and so soon.

He had idolized his father and been completely under his father's guidance. One evening he had bid his father an affectionate good night and thought how strong—yes, even invincible— he was; the next morning they had awakened him with the announcement that his father was dead—murdered—and he was now king!

His grief, the realization of his extreme youth, and the awareness of his vast new burden all combined to produce in him an intense confusion, even panic. Manfully, he tried not to show it, but secretly there was a wild urge to run away, to escape from the terrific responsibility of kingship for which he now felt totally unprepared.

During that dreadful time those about him, shocked and grief-stricken themselves, had not understood what he was going through. It was then that Haman, who had been a mere hanger-on at court, had stepped forward. Haman, who was calm. Haman, who somehow had seemed to know just the right words which would give the bereaved boy the courage and the confidence he so sorely needed at that time.

The fact that Haman was about his father's age, and seemed so wise and so calm, produced in the eighteen-year-old Ahasuerus a curious transference of affection—and Haman, in a way, took his father's place. He could trust Haman as he had trusted his father! How reassuring it had been to the distracted, lonely boy at that time to believe that there was *someone* of all this multitude upon whom he could rely!

Had Ahasuerus not been blinded by the turbulence of this emotional upheaval, he would have seen through Haman promptly and clearly. But now it was too late, for he had one of those natures which, having once given his trust and affection, can see no fault in a friend.

Some people are like that. They will defend a friend, they will shield a friend, they will make excuses for a friend, even though outsiders often wonder why so inferior and superficial a person should merit such devotion. So it was with the young king and Haman.

There was nothing prepossessing about Haman's appearance—a short, thin man with restless, clawlike hands. But he was an adept at flattery, and it almost seemed that he could read the young king's mind, for he never failed to say what Ahasuerus wanted him to say. Now he inwardly rejoiced, not that the king had called him father, but that those standing by had heard it. Now, more than ever, they would fear him.

"As long as the world endures," he said, "the name of Ahasuerus the mighty shall be beloved. What other king could produce so gorgeous a spectacle as this which begins tomorrow and continues for one hundred and eighty-seven days?"

Ahasuerus sighed. "I wish it were over."

Each day he would entertain a new group, and as the state banquet hall was the same area as the throne room—two and a half acres—each day's guests would number into the thousands.

Next morning before his servants came to robe him for the beginning of this historic occasion, the king was alone for a few minutes. His gaze wandered out of the window and rested upon the alabaster palace of his queen. That palace, almost as large as his own, was her domain. There Vashti, an Elamite princess, the most beautiful woman in the world, would entertain the feminine guests. All the world had heard of the beauty of the Persian queen, who lived in her own palace with her own servants and her own high-walled courtyard, never leaving it unless her husband summoned her.

He thought of her now, as proud of her as he was of his other beautiful possessions—haughty and cold, almost as tall as himself and several years his senior. Though there had never been any understanding or companionship between them, there was for him a certain satisfaction in having a wife who was so renowned for her beauty.

This moment of solitude was all that was permitted him. Already he could hear the servants in the corridor outside his door. As they dressed him, putting on the state robes, heavy with embroidery and interwoven with precious stones, he thought of the coming event.

Heretofore the old adage, "As the king does, so do I," had been rigidly adhered to at banquets. So strict had been this observance that guests were compelled to drink only when the king did. He recalled the drunkenness at banquets where his father had presided. He wanted none of that now, so he summoned one of the scribes who always sat outside his door.

"Write this down and see that a copy of it is given to those who will be in service at the feasts. They are not to force anyone to drink by bringing wine continuously as is the custom of the Persians. Everyone is to enjoy himself after his own inclination. Let them cause it to be understood that a man may eat and drink as he pleases, not following what the king does."

When he had given this decree, one of his chief attendants, a man named Bigthan, placed the crown of Persia upon his head. His head was already aching dully, and the crown was heavy, but to have received his guests without it was unthinkable.

The big gates were opening now. The streets of Shushan were crowded as the first contingent of princes and ambassadors, accompanied by their wives and retinues, were carried in elaborate palanquins toward the palace.

At the main gate the women were escorted to the queen's palace, the men were conducted to the throne room where the young king stood surrounded by his bodyguard of ten tall, husky axemen. Introductions proceeded swiftly and with the utmost formality. When the official greetings were over, the inspection of the palace began.

Eyes were envious as they regarded this stalwart young monarch who, having shown them his palace and his treasures, then proceeded to show them the strength of his armies.

Ahasuerus felt very proud that day. He was master of the whole world. The visitors would return to their homelands and say that the lion-king ruled, that he had untold wealth at his command, that his armies were strong, well equipped and well trained. This display would mean, not only peace, but increased trade for Persia.

Day after day the guests came, were impressed, went away to proclaim in their own countries the glories and riches of Persia. At last came the finale. The king was unspeakably weary, his nerves were worn, his eyes were dull from lack of sleep, his smiles were forced.

This was the final feast. The enormous room was lit by five thousand candles. Huge, half-clad Ethiopians with big feathered fans were fanning the air so that the place was cool and there were no flies. The musicians were playing their most beguiling melodies. Dancing girls, clad only in innumerable ropes of beads after the Egyptian fashion, whirled and postured enticingly.

Behind the king's chair stood his two trusted chamberlains, Bigthan and Teresh, whose duty it was to attend to him personally at meals and to sample the food on his plate before placing it before him.

Presently there was a lull in the music, and the dancing girls sank to the floor for an interval of rest. Then a man some distance from Ahasuerus spoke in a loud voice.

"His Majesty shows us his treasures. Ah, but his greatest treasure he keeps hidden from us!"

Another guest, plainly intoxicated, replied sneeringly. "It must be that he knows her loveliness has been exaggerated and she is not so beautiful as they say."

Whereupon another mockingly asked, "What? Could the valiant king of Persia possess anything that was inferior?"

Ahasuerus knew that this conversation was intended for his ears. He knew, too, that had they not been drunk the words would never have been spoken; however, his lean face tightened. All eyes were upon him.

"So!" Haman whispered. "They dare to challenge the king of the Medes and Persians! Impudent mongrels! Does my king wish me to have them expelled?"

The king hesitated. Then he turned to Teresh. "Tell Her Majesty that the king desires her presence. I request her to come before me wearing the royal crown."

The guests forgot their jadedness. There was tension in the air as they waited, eyes expectantly upon the door through which at any moment the world's loveliest woman would appear. Vashti. Her very name meant "beautiful."

As the waiting was prolonged, Ahasuerus became impatient.

The huge room was quiet except for the waving fans.

At length Teresh returned. Standing respectfully beside the king's chair, he waited for the king's nod, which gave him permission to speak.

"The queen sends word that she does not wish to come." The king stiffened. He saw Haman flush with indignation. He saw, too, the guarded smirks, the lifted eyebrows, the meaningful glances which passed among his guests, and here and there an open expression of astonishment.

The voice of Ahasuerus was loaded with authority. "Tell the queen that the king commands her presence."

The messenger went away again. A very deluge of talk began at the banquet table, as though the guests were tactfully trying not to let him know they had heard the queen's reply. He quietly took a sip of wine. He toyed with the sweet on his plate. How dared she? How dared she humiliate him when she knew all the world was looking on? He, the greatest king of the world, could not prove himself master of his own household? Vashti had not only subjected him to the secret derision of the onlookers, but she had actually broken a law which read that a Persian wife must obey her husband.

Again the messenger brought the reply that the queen refused to come. Again among the guests were the half-hidden smiles, the lifted brows, the significant glances.

The king's eyes were hard and bitter. "Tell the queen I command her presence at once!"

There followed a long, uneasy delay. At last, for the third time came the message that Queen Vashti chose not to comply.

The king said nothing more. He turned to the man at his right, asking about shipping conditions in Greece. With a gargantuan effort he waited until a reasonable time had elapsed, then he quietly gave the signal that the banquet was over. The short speech he made was whimsical, gracious, brilliantly clever. He extended to them the courtesy of his kingdom and he wished them all a safe and pleasant journey home.

Finally, when they were all gone, he walked up the stairs to his own room, a lonely and deeply humiliated man. When his servants had taken off the cumbersome robes and the crown they helped him into his embroidered silken night clothes: and he gave them leave to go. At last he was alone.

Walking to a window, he gazed upon the queen's palace.

It was dark as were all the other mansions within the royal walls. Why had she done this thing to him? He could think of but three possible explanations.

One, that Vashti was ambitious and wanted to be queen over an even larger territory, and by openly showing that in reality the king did not have the absolute power attributed to him, the princes of other nations might be tempted to provoke war. Two, he knew that at times Vashti was over-fond of wine. It could be that tonight the wine had made her reckless, imbuing her with the foolhardy courage to defy him, as inwardly perhaps she had longed to do many times in the past. The other reason might be that she had had too much to drink and realized that she was in no condition to be exhibited before the king's guests.

It did not matter what explanation, truth or lie, she might give for her conduct, she was guilty of an unforgivable breach of etiquette and had broken a law. Now for the first time he realized that she had never truly loved him, for had she loved him she would not have humiliated him with the whole world looking on.

His eyes traveled beyond the walls to the sleeping city, sprawling in the moonlight, and he recalled the saying, "As in the king's house, so it is in the kingdom." He knew that by morning Vashti's behavior would be known from one end of the city to the other. It would not stop there. The story would circulate throughout the realm.

Persian women, taught to honor and obey their husbands, would now take their cue from Vashti. They would contend that if the queen could refuse obedience to her husband, they could do likewise. Because of this, homes would be made unhappy, perhaps many disrupted. Besides, what of the ambassadors? They would make their reports.

"Yes," they would say, "we viewed the armies and the arsenals. We saw the wealth of the Persian king. We saw his magnificent stables, his treasures and his trophies, but it was all an empty display, nothing more. A man who cannot rule his own household cannot be so powerful and wise as we think."

So Vashti's refusal would have a deplorable and far-reaching effect. Ahasuerus was angry, but he did not want to act in anger. He was humiliated and unspeakably hurt, yet he wanted to be just. All night he sat in thought. He had loved Vashti, but now, disillusioned, he wondered whether he had really loved her at all. The companionship every normal man wants from his wife he had never known; and now he saw that he never could know it with this woman.

What to do? He had it in his power to put her to death, to exile her, to imprison her. Yet he did not want to be cruel. In her colossal vanity she thought that he loved her so much he would forgive the insult. But he knew that if he forgave and went on as before, it would be condoning her behavior. And that was unthinkable. The whole world was watching. No matter what it cost him, he must act with firmness.

Ahasuerus was calm next morning when he met in session with Haman and his seven councillors. These men were experts in the law, princes of Persia and Media, the wisest men of their time. Sitting at their head was Haman. The men bowed low at the king's entrance, but even as they straightened themselves, they eyed him concernedly, wondering what he would do.

There was old Menucan, a Median. There was Harbonah, the lawyer, who had been admitted as a councillor on the suggestion of Haman. Then there was Carshena, Shothar, Meres, Adrriatha and Marsena.

Haman, speaking for them all, gave the age-old greeting. "O King, live forever!"

Ahasuerus smiled humorously. "You look unhappy, Haman. Too much wine last night?"

"Not so, Your Majesty. I sorrow to burden Your Highness with my domestic troubles, but this morning when breakfast was served, my wife refused to join me. When I sent the servant for her she sent word that she was tired and chose not to rise until it pleased her."

"And I," spoke up Harbonah, "had much the same experience." He gave an eloquent shrug. "As in the house of the king—"

There was a slight and significant pause.

"Your Majesty," said Haman in his suave, oily voice, "last night we who love you looked on and saw you humiliated before the world. You, who sagely rule from India to Ethiopia! The queen made a feast for the women in the royal house. Your Majesty commanded her to come before you wearing the royal crown. She refused. Your humiliation was ours as well. It was the humiliation of every man in the empire."

"My lord the prime minister speaks truly," put in Harbonah. The king, entirely unruffled, looked at them squarely. "What is your advice? What shall I do to Queen Vashti according to the law because she refused to perform the commandment of the King Ahasuerus which he sent to her by the chamberlain?"

Knowing that he loved this woman, they hesitated. They had no reason to love her. She was selfish, ungracious, cruel, capricious, primarily concerned, not with the good of the realm, but with her own incessant adornment.

The king's seeming quietness emboldened them. Haman, toying nervously with his neck chain, spoke in his customary subservient way. "Our beloved king is our guide and model. Behold, the queen's insult to him was an insult to every man in Persia!"

The others nodded. Haman's words were undeniable. The young king sat thoughtful and grave. The queen had sent no apology, so sure was she of her position. He could see her sitting last night, the focal point of attention, and could imagine the wild surge of exultation she must have felt when, before all those women, she boldly affronted their king. In that moment she made a daring boast of her power over him.

"Let us not judge her too harshly," was all that he could find in his heart to say.

"I beg leave," replied Haman, "to bring to Your Majesty's attention the fact that Persian law insists that a wife obey her husband. And may I respectfully remind the king that also according to law it is not for us to accuse the queen."

The king nodded. "It is for me to accuse her to you." In one of his instant transitions of mood, he spoke now in a tone of irritation. "Then I do accuse her! Three times I sent to her. Three times she refused to obey. I therefore give you this order—that you shall inform me what shall be done in regard to her. I state that I shall not receive her as my wife again, but I will have no violence or injustice in this matter."

They knew where they stood now. They need not hedge any longer. He made no excuses for her. This was their cue. Menucan, usually filled with the timidity of the aged, rose and spoke with unwonted vigor.

"The queen has not only done wrong to the king, but to all men living in the king's provinces! For knowledge of her deed shall come abroad. Every woman will know of it. When it is reported that King Ahasuerus commanded his wife to come before him and she refused—why, in the eyes of the women, every husband will be despised! Thus throughout the empire will arise contempt on the part of the women and anger on the part of the men."

The councillors nodded, eyes fixed upon Menucan as though they were supporting the old man by the combined strength of their own wills. Menucan gazed at Ahasuerus to see whether the young ruler was angered. But, his face grim, the king only nodded, thus giving the aged nobleman permission to proceed.

"If it please the king, let there issue a royal commandment from him, and, in order that it may not be altered, let it be written among the laws of the Persians and the Medes—that Vashti come no more before the king! When this is published throughout the king's vast empire, all wives shall give their husbands honor!"

Menucan sat down, amazed at his own daring.

Ahasuerus sought to postpone the inevitable announcement.

"I would hear another voice on the matter."

Haman rose."May it please the king." He cleared his throat. "I agree with Prince Menucan. This affront has been offered not to the king alone but to all Persians, who, by the queen's act, are now in danger of being disobeyed by their wives."

"True." Harbonah nodded.

"So be it," replied the king. "This day be it written that a bill of divorcement is now in effect against the former queen, and that the king decrees that every man shall rule in his own house!"

The former queen! Vashti was no longer queen of Persia! The scribes, always present at councils, proceeded to record the bill of divorcement. Since Vashti had refused to obey the king's summons she was commanded never to approach him or even communicate with him in the future.

She was ordered to move from the queen's palace at once and take her abode in a small guest house on the property. This house, though within the walls of the vast grounds, was so far removed from the king's residence that he would never see it unless he visited it.

Weary, troubled, the king left the room. He had been fond of Vashti, yet he knew that under Persian law, after taking these steps, reconciliation was impossible. The law was the law. Even he could not break a law. Besides, to attempt reconciliation would betray weakness. And that a king must never do.

Vashti had been so sure of her power that the news came as a complete surprise. To live in that comparatively small house! She would have her own courtyard, but who would enter it? No longer queen, no one would visit her, for now they had nothing to gain by doing so. And only last night a thousand women had fawned upon her!

She had thought it wonderful to show those adoring women that she was not subservient to her husband! She had reveled in their shocked gasps when she sent that arrogant message. And now her day of splendor was over. Yet—was she not the most beautiful woman in the world? Let him try to find anyone to compare with her!

She had never loved him, therefore the loss of his love brought no pain. But that she had lost her position as queen over the greatest kingdom on earth, that was unbearable!

After nightfall, attended by the comparatively few maidservants and eunuchs who had been allotted to her, Vashti left the queen's palace and entered the house which formerly had been used only for the chief servants of visiting dignitaries. Here she would live until she died, lonely, unloved—a forgotten woman.

As weeks passed, the king tried to lose himself in the mountain of official business which always confronted him.

He wanted love. He shunned close friendships. Experience had taught him to mistrust everyone—except Haman. He was a powerful monarch, yet he had no one in the world to love him for himself alone.

When three years had passed, the councillors began to worry about him. Finally when Menucan, Harbonah and Haman were dining with him one night, Menucan spoke gently.

"I think Your Majesty still remembers fondly Vashti who was once his queen."

"It is true," said Ahasuerus.

Haman spoke soothingly. "0 King, if I am too bold, forgive me. My concern is based upon my love for you. Forget Vashti. She was never worthy."

"Forget her? How?"

"Another wife," said Harbonah. "Another love. I pray Your Majesty to let us send abroad over all the empire and search out beautiful maidens. Let them be brought here. Let the king see them, one by one. Let him choose which he considers most likely to give him happiness."

"His Majesty was but a boy when his marriage with Vashti was arranged for him," put in Haman. "He is now twenty-four, capable of giving a man's love to a woman."

"Aye." Harbonah nodded, always alert to echo Haman. "Let there be lovely virgins sought for the king. Let us appoint officers in every province to gather together all the fair young damsels, sending the best to the palace. Let them be brought to The House of the Women and put in the custody of Hegai, the chamberlain. And let the maiden who pleases the king be queen!"

The king considered the suggestion lengthily. For a time he stared out of the window, his eyes upon an avenue of fig trees.

"So be it," he declared at last.

"Good!" exclaimed Haman.

Ahasuerus waved a bored hand. "But don't trouble me with details. Let every maid be escorted by a score of soldiers for her protection on the way. Send three people—a middle-aged woman and two eunuchs—to each province. Let her be under their care. See to it that there does not enter into this matter such things as high or low birth, of much or little money, or of religion. For the rest, my lords, conduct the affair as it pleases .you."

They smiled. Menucan rose, lifting his goblet in mid-air. "To the new queen of Persia!"

"To our future queen!" cried Haman.

3: Beauty Contest in Babylon

HADASSAH was seventeen, and Mordecai could no longer delay finding her a husband. He knew that he was being criticized, but he had never permitted himself to be swayed by the opinions of others.

As for Hadassah, she was deeply humiliated, thinking that no one had spoken for her. Her friends were now all married and they looked at her with pity. "Poor Hadassah!" they sighed. No man has asked her for his son! Poor thing!"

They had been shocked at the news of the king's divorce. Even the women had been loud in declaring that the arrogant Vashti got just what she deserved, and after a few weeks no one spoke of her any more. No one cared now what colors she wore.

On an evening in spring, Mordecai was walking homeward, his mind engrossed in the weighty problem of Hadassah's marriage.

That day two eligible men had asked for her and he was trying to choose which would be suitable. Even as he considered the matter, he heard the official trumpets and, instead of going home, turned in the direction of the sound.

The announcement came simultaneously with Mordecai's arrival at The Place of Assembly.

"Be it known to the citizens of Babylon! The all-wise king, Ahasuerus the lion-hearted, has decided to choose a wife. The consort worthy of our noble king must be the most beautiful virgin in the empire. She must be freeborn, not a slave. By order of His Majesty and the governor of this province, every able-bodied damsel between the ages of fourteen and eighteen is commanded to report at sunrise tomorrow at the side gate of the *kasr*. Babylon hopes to have the honor of sending to the royal palace at Shushan the one who will be the future queen of Persia and Media!"

As Mordecai turned homeward he realized that the order included Hadassah. In a way, he was relieved that this decree would postpone the necessity of choosing her bridegroom, for until a girl had been dismissed from the contest, no parent or guardian would dare negotiate an espousal.

Arriving home, he found the old woman and his niece palpably excited. Hadassah s face was more vivacious than he had seen it for a long time.

"But of course, I shall only have to report" she was saying. "Sit down," ordered the old woman. "You must be unwearied for tomorrow. You must not burn your hands. Get away from the fire. Heat toughens the skin. Sit down and be quiet. Who knows? You may be the next queen of Persia!"

Hadassah laughed merrily at that, and since she had one of the most infectious laughs in the world, the glum old woman was presently chuckling with her.

"Me! Queen of Persia!"

"And why not?" said Mordecai from the doorway.

"Uncle Mordecai! I did not hear you come in. Wait now, let me get your clean sandals."

"And would the possible next queen of Persia serve her tired old uncle?"

She blushed happily. "Oh, now you are joking again."

His smile faded. 'Would you like to be queen?"

"I? I? Why—why—oh, but I—"

"You have always been queen of my household," he said solemnly. "And there is royal blood in you. I have taught you to walk, to talk, to behave in such a way that you would grace even the great palace at Shushan. And you are beautiful."

She blushed, all confused, not knowing how to reply, for never before had he told her she was beautiful. He regarded her critically, as a judge might do. In this past year she had bloomed into lovely womanhood. Her figure was smooth, slender, symmetrical—girlish and yet stately. Her feet, shod now in house sandals, were dainty and patrician. Her flesh was delicate and flawless, with a faint peach-like hue on the cheeks. She used no kohl around her eyes and she needed none, for her lashes were silky, upcurling and dark.

Her brows were dark, level, well defined, as though they had been painted in ink by some masterly hand. Her mouth, naturally red, was one of the most exquisite he had ever seen. Her teeth were white and glistening. She had the knack of falling into entrancing postures. Yes, this niece of his had a chance.

"Tomorrow," said the old woman, breaking in upon his inspection, "our Hadassah will compete with the most beautiful damsels in Babylon, and everybody knows that Babylon is noted for its beautiful women. What will you wear, little mistress?"

"I have few jewels, but"—Hadassah's face lit up with eagerness—"I could borrow some from Sarah and Rebecca."

The old woman nodded excitedly.

"You will wear none," ordered Mordecai.

"No jewels, master?" gasped the old woman. "Why, there will be damsels there wearing the richest ornaments, and what are jewels for except to enhance a woman's appearance?"

"No jewels, no cosmetics."

"Is it," asked Hadassah simply, "that my uncle does not wish me to be chosen?"

She was always like that, direct and honest, never the sort to prattle as most girls of her age, and never resorting to the artifice of tears and pouts to get her own way. He knew that she naturally would have liked to bedeck herself in the best she had, and left to herself, would surely borrow some baubles from her wealthier friends.

"As to whether I wish you to be chosen, I do not know," he admitted. "One Babylonian damsel will be selected to go to Shushan. But that does not mean that this maiden will be the king's choice. Naturally, Babylon would be honored to have its contestant wear the crown. I am not sure that I would like to see you queen of Persia, my child. I am not socially ambitious. I desire only your happiness. Tell me, how do you yourself feel about it?"

"Sir, indeed I scarcely know. It has happened so suddenly." She laughed, excited again. "I suppose this night every girl in Babylon is dreaming of being queen."

"It is no disgrace to be rejected by the judges," he reminded her, attempting to prepare her for such a possibility.

"I suppose I shall have to compete?"

"It is an order," he answered.

At the evening meal they spoke seldom, Hadassah trying to imagine what awaited her next day.

She knew that at this moment throughout Babylon, every girl who was eligible was planning what she would wear, was bathing and anointing herself. She had no conviction that she would win, but it was her duty to report. So, the meal over, she washed her long hair, stroked it with her palms, brushed and anointed it. Then she bathed, cleaned and cut her nails and laid out her best robes, running to her uncle and asking his opinion as to which was most becoming.

But he only said of each that it was "very nice." Finally, realizing that he was giving her no help in a matter which she obviously considered of paramount importance, he said, "Wear the one you feel best in. The most beautiful woman in the world would appear less lovely if she were uncomfortable and ill at ease."

"And no jewels? Not even a ring and a neckchain?"

He smiled amusedly. "They will not be looking at your jewelry. In fact, it might even detract. I have always thought that the exquisite line of a young, firm throat is marred by the heavy neckchains that are so fashionable nowadays."

She did not argue. She took his advice humbly, and seating herself in a chair facing him, she muttered dreamily, “I have always wanted to see the king. Just to see him. I remember the time of his coronation six years ago. I was eleven then, and I used to lie in my bed at night imagining him passing close to me and smiling at me, and—" she confessed in her artless way, smiling a little as though she knew it was absurd, "I still think of him and still dream of meeting him face to face. And now—why, now I am almost afraid to see him for fear that he may be less than I imagined him. And to be queen! Oh, no! Foolish as my dreams were, they never soared as high as that!"

Next morning, with Mordecai beside her, she walked out of the Hebrew quarter. Laborers and slaves, those whose occupations prevented them from going in the vicinity of the palace, smiled and waved, wishing the veiled, slight figure good fortune. An atmosphere of friendliness and animation prevailed throughout that fabulous, colorful Babylon which was called "the land of the Chaldeans."

Situated on both banks of the river Euphrates, the city, surrounded by lofty walls, spread out for over a hundred square miles. It was sliced through by the river, its two parts connected by a stone bridge which was over one thousand yards in length and thirty feet wide. Two royal palaces faced each other majestically on each side of the bridge, connected by a tunnel underneath the river.

Mordecai and Hadassah were crossing the bridge now, walking rapidly, part of the excited tempo of a crowd in a holiday mood. Rich and poor hoped to witness the choosing of the city's most perfect specimen of femininity.

Now Mordecai and Hadassah were turning into The Sacred Way which was even more crowded than the side streets. The vast throng moved jauntily in the direction of the *kasr*, or palace of old King Nebuchaddnezzar, which was still kept in excellent repair and was now the official state building—the city hall.

This was an impressive edifice with the famous hanging gardens adjoining it. The route taken by Mordecai and his niece led them past the Tower of Babel, which, though destroyed soon after its completion, still remained, a vast mound of bricks, and one of the places of historical interest.

When the people reached the *kasr*, they were disappointed to discover that the beauty contest would take place in the privacy of the rear courtyard which was enclosed by high walls.

Even the relatives of the contestants were not permitted to accompany them inside. They must wait outside with the crowd, which, disgruntled at not being admitted, nevertheless milled about, excitedly discussing the event, and pushing and shoving for glimpses of the contestants.

Mordecai gave Hadassah a reassuring pat on the arm as she took leave of him. “Your name;” he said as a reminder, "is Esther."

She smiled, grateful to him for recalling this to her, for she was so accustomed to being addressed as Hadassah that without his warning she would certainly have given the wrong name.

"You will wait for me?" she asked, somewhat plaintively. "Oh, yes," he replied, off-handedly as if this should have been understood.

She smiled humorously. "You won't have to wait long." He shrugged, as though it did not matter one way or the other. "When you get inside, remove your veil."

A soldier opened the gate, holding it ajar wordlessly as she passed him.

Inside the court a platform had been built. Before it, shaded by awnings were seats for the judges. There was the governor of the province and his staff, and a group of scribes in readiness to take notes of the proceedings.

With the exception of three people—a dignified woman in her forties and two men—all were Babylonians. Esther knew at once that these three who seemed to be in charge, had come from Shushan because they did not wear what strangers called "the babylonish garment." Their clothes, though rich, were not cut upon the ample lines worn by natives of Babylonia.

Hadassah—who kept reminding herself to give her name as Esther—turned her attention to her fellow-contestants.

Since Babylon was a city of mixed races, these girls were of widely differing types. Like Esther, most of them wore capes, extremely full, falling gracefully over one shoulder and caught up on the other side at the center of the belt. Esther wore her hair in braids, but many of the other girls had elaborate coiffures; especially evidenced was the ultra-smart catogen, made more spectacular by colored bands or many large, knobbed pins. Earrings, bracelets and brooches were also large, and arms and legs were often almost entirely covered by bracelets of gold or beads of agate, lapis, onyx or carnelian.

There were many benches, on the edges of these the girls nervously seated themselves. Some were tall, some short, some fat, others thin. Some were sumptuously gowned, heavily scented, others were poorly clothed. Some were ridiculously overdressed, and their innumerable anklets and bracelets made jingling sounds as they walked. Esther began to suspect that these tinkling ornaments had been donned because the wearers hoped that their noise would attract attention to themselves.

It was about eight in the morning when a stout man—one of the three Shushanites—announced that the contestants were to form in line at the right of the platform. Most of the girls, eager to be among the first, rushed forward, some pushing others out of the way. One girl screamed that another had stepped on her toe and crushed it.

The stout man frowned and said, "Quiet! Quiet!"

Esther rose from her bench unhurriedly and was therefore among those at the end of the line. Like the others, she now busied herself smoothing her hair, her robe, adjusting a neckline.

The girl in front of her took a mirror from a little pouch she carried, and stared concernedly into it for a long time. Then she replaced the mirror and took from the pouch a vial of perfume, dousing herself with it until the air around her was odorous with a heavy, sickeningly sweet scent.

Now the contest began. The stout man stood guard, letting each girl mount the platform alone. Some were speedily dismissed, often leaving the courtyard in tears. Hour after hour passed while the line moved now slow, now fast. Occasionally he told a girl to report tomorrow.

If the stout man deemed a girl worthy of consideration, he called out to her to sit, to smile, to walk back and forth a few times, to turn around, to lift her arms.

At noon the line was half as long as it had been in the beginning, and a respite was called for the midday meal.

Those who had not yet been seen were hot and tired and they returned to the benches under the trees where they were served with fruit, bread, cheese and watered wine.

The beauty of Babylon was on parade that day. Hadassah, who only twice before had left the Hebrew quarter, was now seeing the unveiled loveliness of Hebrew maidens, Egyptians, Chaldeans and Amalekites. She considered them all more entrancing than herself, admiring the bearing of the Egyptians with their long, slim necks, white linen robes, clipped hair and hennaed nails; and the dark, insolent, fleshly beauty of the Amalekites.

What an amazing thing it was, she thought, that this identical contest was being repeated in every province of the empire! In each city, in each country district, girls like these in the courtyard, were undergoing this same observation. They would gather in some place like this, generally overdressed, some in borrowed finery, some wearing scarves whose long fringes denoted their rank as princesses.

Esther realized now how shielded she had always been, and how little Mordecai cared for display, preferring to give his money to charity or spend it upon books. Not that they had ever lacked anything in Mordecai's household. She had had a happy childhood. Surely, even had she been reared in a king's court she could not have been happier.

The girl on the bench beside her was twitching restlessly.

"How can you sit there so quietly?" she fumed at last.

Esther smiled, remembering how Uncle Mordecai had taught her to sit quietly, often for an hour at a time, because he said that of all things he disliked "a fidgety woman."

Now came the sound of trumpets announcing the arrival of the dignitaries, who took their seats. The courtyard was amazingly still as those contestants who had not yet been judged, formed in line. Hadassah, to her dismay, was almost at the beginning. She had been calm until now, looking on as an interested spectator, but now she found herself wildly impelled to dash for the gate. She was weary, and her palms were damp with perspiration.

So slowly did the line move that it was an hour before her turn came, and oddly when she stepped upon the platform all trepidation departed. It was strange that she whose life had been wholly free from pomp and who never appeared in public without her veil, could have walked with such composure upon the platform. She did what the stout man ordered. She sat, and they noted that she sat easily, her well-groomed hands relaxed, her chin slightly elevated.

"Smile, damsel."

She smiled, and they noted the shine of her white teeth "Rise and turn."

She turned, and they noted the way she held her shoulders and the trim, tapering line of her torso.

"Damsel, walk back and forth three times."

She walked, and they noted the graceful swing of her body.

One of the judges whispered to another that this girl moved as if to music. But their faces were inscrutable.

The fat man motioned her off the platform and summoned the next contestant. His fellow Shushanite sat at a small table on the left side of the platform.

"Your name?" he asked as she neared him.

"Esther."

"Age?"

"Seventeen. "

"Tomorrow midmorn you will return. Come to the side gate. This tablet will admit you."

Exhausted with the ordeal, she hurried from the court to find Mordecai patiently waiting outside the gate. The crowd had grown weary with the heat and the sun, and there remained only a few relatives of the girls who were still to be judged.

"Well?" asked her uncle.

She shrugged. "I was told to return tomorrow." She told him all that had happened.

"Even not to have been dismissed at once is an honor," he said when she had finished. "But you must not expect too much. Consider the extent of the Persian empire—from India on the east to Thrace and Egypt on the west, and on the south to the Indian Ocean, the Arabian desert and the Persian Gulf; on the north it includes the whole of eastern Asia between the Black Sea, the Caucasus, the Caspian Sea and the Jaxartes. It is impossible for a damsel like you to imagine so vast a territory."

She nodded. "Truly, I'm not foolish enough to imagine that I shall be queen. I shall not be disappointed if I'm dismissed tomorrow."

Arriving home they found the old woman concocting a paste of powdered henna leaves. "I heard that some of the contestants were told to come back tomorrow," she explained. "I thought, in case you were one of them, I'd have this ready. It's to tint your nails and the tips of your fingers."

"Oh, thank you!" And Hadassah told the old woman all that had happened.

Next day, her finger tips and nails painted, Hadassah crossed the bridge beside her uncle. He was walking slowly and thoughtfully, seeming in no hurry to deliver her at the gate. In fact, he even stopped for a few minutes to observe a hairdresser who was making curls of artificial hair.

"Curls for your lady?" asked the man. "I can match her hair exactly."

Mordecai shook his head and went on. But now they had to pause again because of a procession. The Babylonians had these religious processions frequently. The white-robed priests carried their gods through the streets as a reminder to the worldly Babylonians to attend the temples.

There was no crowd moving in the direction of the *kasr* now.

People knew that they would not be admitted, and so they returned to their occupations, pausing to ask of passers-by, "Have you heard whether the affair at the *kasr* is settled yet?"

When Esther entered the grounds she found that out of the hundreds of contestants, only about fifty had been commanded to return. Again there were the judges, but now they were not seated.

As each girl stepped on the platform they walked around her, peering at her nails and teeth, looking closely at her skin, hair, eyes. Esther found this close inspection embarrassing. She blushed and wanted desperately to get away. The heat was stifling, yet she was cold and hot by turns.

Her ordeal over, she was told to return next day.

When she told this to Mordecai, he smiled. She could see that he was pleased. After all, wasn't this girl his handiwork? Had he this long while been unwittingly training her to wear a crown, fitting her to dwell amidst the untold luxury of the Persian court? Could it be that his Hadassah—? He looked down at her concernedly. What did she know about the Persians? She had never even met one. He began to talk of them, preparing her for what he now thought was bound to come.

"You will like and respect the Persians. True, they are more concerned with the pleasures of the table than we are, but they are highly intelligent, sophisticated, witty, generous. Their minds are quick and keen. In war they're brave and reckless. We Hebrews have cause to love them, because when they conquered Babylonia they found us here, not permitted to leave the country, still captives and slaves. They gave us freedom to settle where we chose. They showed us special consideration, I think, because like ourselves they do not worship idols, and in their temples are neither altars nor images. I'm told that Shushan is one of the most beautiful cities in the world. The air there is dry and bracing. One can see immense distances because of the clarity of the atmosphere and at night the stars seem so close that it is almost as if one might reach up and touch them."

Hadassah regarded her uncle in astonishment. "You speak," she said in her direct and candid way, "as if I were really going to Shushan!"

Not knowing how she felt in the matter, he answered guardedly. "I am beginning to consider it a possibility."

Her face grew tense and white. Could it be? Could it really happen—to her? The prospect was at once marvelous and terrifying. Mordecai noticed that her step grew buoyant and then after a time it slowed down. Could it be, she kept asking herself, that she would really see the king?

Next day when she entered the court she saw that the platform had been taken down and a tent had been set up. The governor and the princes were no longer in evidence. This time there were only twenty girls, all curious as to what would confront them in the tent.

The first to enter was a Chaldean who wore a robe richly embroidered with astronomical signs. After ten minutes she emerged, her face brick-red, eyes glaring, hurrying angrily out of the courtyard. The next, a Hebrew girl, remained inside about twenty minutes. When she left, her face was ash-white and her hands were clenched.

Now it was Esther's turn.

Inside the tent she found three women. Two were servants. The other was the middle-aged Shushanite, who ordered the servants to help Esther undress. When the girl stood naked and uncomfortable, the Shushanite inspected every part of her body. She knelt, taking each foot in her hands, noticing the straightness and symmetry of the toes, the height of the insteps, the curve of the arches. She examined Esther's body for scars and birthmarks. She looked closely into her ears, her eyes. Then she told Esther to open her mouth. Now she peered at her teeth.

Silently and with an impassive face, the Shushanite touched Esther's skin to judge its smoothness. She felt her arms to estimate their firmness. She inspected her elbows to see that they were not discolored or callused. She unbraided Esther's hair and inspected her scalp, on the alert for abrasions and dandruff. Then she asked her to speak and noted the beautiful timbre of her voice.

"Help her put on her robes."

As the servants obeyed, the Shushanite stood, making notes on a clay tablet. She was a tall, slender woman with iron-gray hair and a kind, homely face.

"Wait outside," she said crisply at last, and ordered a servant to summon the next contestant.

Esther walked into the sunlight, embarrassed by the minuteness of this inspection and wishing now that she had been among those dismissed the first day. Finding a bench, she sank upon it, holding her veil in her hands. She shuddered at the thought that she might have to endure such a thing again. She was nervous now, wondering how much longer this would go on. Some of the girls came quickly from the tent as the close inspection of the keen-eyed Shushanite woman revealed some hitherto hidden flaw.

Now the last girl was leaving the tent, vainly trying to control her hands and a nervous twitching of her painted lips.

Five girls remained. Now the Shushanite woman told them to come with her. Wordlessly, they followed her into the palace. Here, in a large room, the judges were seated. The two Shushanite men were standing. To them the Shushanite woman presented her reports, which they studied while the girls waited. Then they passed the reports to the judges.

When the judges had read them, the five girls were told to line up side by side. Two of them were quickly eliminated. The task of the judges was more difficult now. But finally the other two were motioned away.

Esther stood alone.

The judges were smiling, the three Shushanites were smiling—everyone was suddenly smiling.

The governor rose and bowed before Esther. "Babylon has made its choice."

For a moment she thought she was going to faint. But Mordecai's discipline made it possible for her to accept the statement with outward dignity, even apparent serenity.

"We are convinced," went on the governor, "that in Esther, Babylon will never know shame. We send you to Shushan proudly. This night you may spend with your family. Tomorrow morning your name will be proclaimed. Before the announcement, at the hour before dawn, you will report here.

Bring only such things as you will need for the journey, for from here you will leave for Shushan."

She nodded; then, followed by the two men from Shushan, she turned and left the room.

4: Farewell to Babylon

MORDECAI, looking a trifle worn with the strain and the heat and the hours of standing, was awaiting Esther as, escorted by the two fat men, she left the palace grounds.

"This lady is your daughter?" asked the taller man.

"My niece. She has no parents."

"She is the choice. May she wear the crown!"

"I am honored," replied Mordecai, "but not surprised."

"She leaves tomorrow for Shushan. Have no fear for her safety. She will be well protected. The woman who inspected her in the privacy of the tent will be her personal maid. We"—he indicated the other man—"will be in attendance. My colleague's name is Sabuchadas. Mine is Acratheus. We are eunuchs in the service of the king. In addition to the three of us, your niece will be accompanied by an escort of soldiers. So you may be assured that she will reach Shushan safely."

"It is kind of you, sir, to tell me these things. I would naturally be concerned. And if she fails to please the king?"

"His Majesty has decreed that those who wish to return to their homes are free to do so, and the second journey will be in precisely the same manner as the first. So we will either bring the damsel back to you or—we will have the honor of serving her as queen."

"So be it," replied Mordecai.

He bowed, the men bowed. Then through the now deepening gloom, he and his niece walked toward the Hebrew section.

Trembling, weak and frightened, Esther clung to her uncle's arm.

He smiled. "So! I am walking beside the most beautiful maiden in Babylon!"

She gazed up at him, thinking how this man had protected her, trained her and cared for her. How would she get along without him in that strange foreign place?

"How can you be so cheerful?" she asked faintly. "Tomorrow I shall go away! I—I am afraid!"

"Your alarm is natural, but—now I am very serious. Listen closely. When you go to the house of the king, you will eat what is set before you, never asking whether or not it is kosher. If you are chosen, you must know that your position demands that you be bigger than any restriction of a particular people, for all the races gathered in the whole empire will be your people. Have they asked about your religion?"

"They asked nothing but my name and age."

"Things will be hard enough for you. You must not make them harder. From now on you are not Hadassah. You are Esther."

She sighed. Were the days of Hadassah over forever? Esther sounded dignified and strange. Hadassah sounded natural.

Arriving at the house, they found it filled with friends. A very torrent of talk had been going on, but as Mordecai opened the door it ceased abruptly.

Sarah rushed up to her, speaking effusively. "Hadassah! We heard you were among the last! What an honor!"

Mordecai faced them. "Hadassah has been chosen!" Chosen! They gazed at her now as though they had never seen her before. Her face flushed a little under their concerted scrutiny. There was a long, uneasy silence.

"She leaves for the king's palace tomorrow," went on Mordecai.

"So? So? Is it so?" asked someone. "Tomorrow?" gasped Sarah.

This girl standing there so tiredly before them, this girl whom they had known all their lives, could it be that she would be their queen? The news seemed to distress them. They did not know how to act or what to say. They were confused, agitated.

Standing by Mordecai's side, sensing the chasm that was even now widening between her and her people, Hadassah felt suddenly lonely and terrified.

Her friends were looking at her in a new way. They were saying, "Can it be that she will rule over us?" For a wild moment she wanted to hide from those peering eyes, wanted to go back to being just Hadassah again.

"Tomorrow she goes?" asked a man's voice out of the crowd. "Tomorrow."

One would have thought that they would have been tactful enough to leave after knowing that, but instead they stayed, suddenly embarrassed in the presence of this girl. Then all the women crowded about her, each offering excitedly to contribute some article of apparel to augment her own wardrobe. They insisted that they would feel honored if she would accept these gifts. They grew loud and stubborn about it when Hadassah kept telling them that she had been ordered to bring only enough for the journey.

"It is a long journey!" said the old woman.

And now everyone began discussing how long the journey was.

Hadassah looked into Sarah's eyes. Last week there had been pity, even superiority in them because no man had spoken for her. Tonight there was envy.

Sarah tried to speak lightly. "It is a great honor, that you have been chosen out of all the damsels in Babylon. It makes me proud to say that we grew up together, but do not feel disgraced if His Majesty sends you home again."

Before Hadassah could reply, Mordecai spoke. "It is true that she may return. But it is possible that she may not. In either case, Hadassah is going into a strange country, among strangers. So far no inquiries have been made as to her religion. We know that her position will be difficult enough, and we know that it will be even more difficult for her than it would be for a Chaldean or a Thracian, an Egyptian or a Median, because the prime minister is an Amalekite."

There were quick murmurs of agreement. The sense of estrangement between themselves .and this girl was suddenly dissipated. In an instant they were unified, each wanting to protect this member of their own race.

Sensing their changed attitude, Mordecai spoke quickly. "If we want to protect her, we will never let it be known that she lived in this quarter."

A rabbi spoke up. "We all know how you feel. The Amalekite would prejudice the king against her. We Hebrews have already suffered too much from the hands of this unscrupulous Arab tribe which boasts that it is Aryan. It is our duty to protect each other in every possible way, and we can protect Hadassah by keeping silence as to her religion."

The others agreed.

When at last they left, Hadassah and Mordecai faced each other, and she saw that there was heartache in him.

But he did not voice it. He turned to the old woman. "Pack her things. Only what she will need on the journey."

"I may come back," Hadassah murmured, when the servant had gone.

"And you may not. For the first time in your life you will be among people who are not of your religion. Thank God, here in Persia no one is persecuted because of his faith. But say nothing about being a Hebrew. However, if you are asked, do not lie. And though you will no longer keep the Sabbath or attend synagogue, you are not to forget your prayers.

"My uncle is wise," she replied meekly. "I will obey as I have always done."

"And now you must go to bed and try to sleep."

"But—what will you do without me?"

He spoke lightly. "Do not worry about your old uncle. I shall manage quite well. No more talk now. Bless you. Good night."

In her room, Hadassah, who a few minutes ago had been so tired that she thought she would faint, now felt no tiredness whatever. She knew that she should be elated at such good fortune, yet she felt frightened and dreaded the daylight. She prayed for strength, for inner calmness, and finally she stumbled into bed.

Two hours before dawn she rose and was ready for departure when the servant summoned her to breakfast. Mordecai said his customary morning prayer before the meal, but when they began to eat, neither of them spoke. The old woman was silent, too. When the meal was over and Hadassah turned to bid her good-by, she burst into tears and ran into the courtyard.

"We must be going," said Mordecai quietly.

Hadassah picked up her small bundle, and she and her uncle left the house. They walked rapidly, Mordecai holding himself even more erect than usual. He led her by way of the side streets which were almost empty at this hour. A roseate glow nudged the sky gently, but as they walked it widened and intensified into red-gold glory, touching the splendid temples and ornate villas, and causing the date palms to stand out in bold contrast, like silhouettes. A woman passed them carrying on her head a heavy, brightly painted water jar, the expensive kind that came from Greece. Now they passed a brickyard, where laborers were already mixing the clay with straw and adding sand with all the absorption of a painstaking cook mixing cakes. A sorcerer stood in a doorway, swinging his censer. His eyes were closed and he was mumbling a series of syllables in a monotonous, toneless drawl. There were many sorcerers in Babylon and many astrologers. They claimed the power to read one's fate in the stars and to exorcise every phase of evil.

"I wonder what he would foretell for me," murmured Hadassah.

"I do not believe in such things," replied Mordecai shortly. She gazed up at him, realizing that in a little while she would bid him good-by. As always he was tastefully dressed, with carefully tended prayer curls on either side of his face, the ritual purple tassels at the four corners of his coat, a gold bracelet on his left arm, rings of carnelian and agate on his long fingers, and a necklace of lapis lazuli.

She knew that though this morning he had dressed with his usual care, he was nevertheless going through a sharp inner struggle, a struggle so intense that he found speech difficult, for if one talks at such times, the struggle inevitably betrays itself, and speech might even end in tears.

How can I say good-by to him without sobbing and making a scene? thought Hadassah. But inwardly she was weeping. All darkness had gone from the sky now, but the glory had gone, too, and there was only a tranquil blue vault and a steadily glaring sun.

"It will be hot today," said Mordecai casually.

Hadassah did not answer. They were nearing the entrance. of the palace courtyard now, and her face paled at the realization that in a moment the parting must come.

"Lift your veil," said her uncle.

She obeyed. Reaching the gate they stood, hearts too torn to know how to face this parting. Her lips quivered childishly. She began to tremble. Mordecai's face was white and he looked at her sternly.

"A queen does not cry."

"I am not yet a queen. I may never be a queen. I am thinking how good you have always been to me. And now I am frightened. When I was a little girl and something frightened me, I used to run to you, and you would talk to me and tell me there was nothing to be afraid of and make me laugh at my fears, and give me almonds because you knew I loved them—"

She was interrupted by the opening of the gate. Acratheus stood within it, as though he had been posted there to watch for her. Both she and Mordecai were relieved at the appearance of this stranger.

"Lady, I have been waiting for you," he said, and then addressed Mordecai. "Only this far can you go, sir."

Mordecai nodded. "My name is Mordecai. I am her only relative. If anything amiss befalls her, will you promise to communicate with me? You will have no trouble finding me. I am well known in the—the Hebrew quarter."

"Oh? The Hebrew quarter? Yes, I might have known that from the tassels on your coat. But the name, it is a Babylonian name, not Hebrew. Esther, too, is a Babylonian name."

Mordecai's shrewd eyes were gauging this man. "There have been no questions asked concerning her religion."

Acratheus smiled. "And there will be none. You need have no anxiety on that score. As for me, I received my training from childhood in the king's palace, and I learned early to keep my mouth shut. Come then, lady. Do not be afraid. His Majesty is kind. You have nothing to fear."

She looked at Mordecai, who was standing white-faced and grim. Solemnly now, he kissed her on the forehead. "My blessings go with you. May God watch—between you and me—until—until we meet—again."

Acratheus took her arm and gently led her inside the gate.

Then the gate closed with a decisive bang as though it were forever shutting her off from her uncle and her old friends and her old life.

Eyes downcast, fighting desperately against tears, she continued along the path with her tall companion, who, without speaking, relieved her of her bundle. He led her through a broad garden and into the ancient palace, along a thickly carpeted corridor. He permitted her no time to look around, and presently he opened a door, announcing to someone inside, "Here she is!" Then he closed the door and Esther was alone with the strange Shushanite woman.

Outside, from the palace turret and at the various Places of Assembly throughout the city, the trumpeters were summoning the inhabitants of Babylon, and the officials were mounting the marble platforms to announce that the contest had ended.

Babylon was sending to His Majesty Ahasuerus, king of the Medes and Persians, a native of this city named Esther. The announcers in glowing terms extolled her beauty, her grace, her charm, her freshness, and expressed the fervent hope that Babylon's choice would be their next queen. Esther was to leave in an hour for Shushan.

The speech was followed by wild cheers and the clapping of hands. No sooner had the cheers and the hand clapping subsided than everyone hastened breathlessly to the palace to see, if possible, this hitherto unknown girl named Esther who now, in some curious way, seemed to belong to all of them and who perhaps would have bestowed upon her the highest honor in the land.

Meanwhile, in the quiet room at the palace, the middle-aged woman who had inspected her in the tent, rose and greeted Esther with a low bow. Her manner was no longer brusque and impersonal. It was sympathetic, it was respectful, it was even motherly. Somehow it managed to have an air half servant, half friend.

"I am Malme. I am in service at the palace at Shushan and came thither with the two eunuchs, Acratheus and Sabuchadas, to conduct to the capitol the chosen one."

Esther was quick thinking and intuitive. At once she knew that Malme, Acratheus and Sabuchadas would be both mentors and servitors. They would serve her, yet she was expected to obey them. Though middle-aged and an upper servant, Malme was smartly dressed. The iron-gray hair was coiffed in Assyrian style, with innumerable tiny curls. She used eye shadow, her lips were painted, her finger and toenails were hennaed, and she carried a feather fan. Attempting to put Esther at ease, she began to talk of the fan.

"I never use one in Shushan, but oh, this fearful Babylonian heat! How do you people stand it? But I suppose I should say nothing against Babylonia." She smiled amusedly. "Ah, you Babylonians! Confirmed boasters, all of you. No country on earth is as fertile as Babylonia, no figs are as sweet as your figs. No grapes are as juicy, no pomegranates are as luscious, no melons as succulent, no dates are as large. You Babylonians are all alike. We Shushanites really have to laugh. We can be sure that immediately after meeting a Babylonian, he will begin boasting about his country and its canals and its scenery."

"I suppose we are as you say. Tell me, to each province in the empire went three representatives of the king?"

"That is so. Three were chosen for each candidate, three who were deemed worthy to oversee the matter and conduct the chosen one to Shushan. In addition there will be soldiers to guard each damsel on the way."

After a short pause, Esther asked, "Shall I—shall I see Vashti?"

"No one ever sees Vashti, no one ever mentions her. Once we looked up to her, but now we know she was a fool. Why should she have refused to obey her lord? It's not unusual for Persian nobles to have their wives present at feasts. Let us hope that the next queen—whosoever she may be—will not make such mistakes. Are you hungry? Would you like some food before starting?"

"I am sure I could eat nothing."

"You do not seem elated at this honor."

"I—it is all so strange. It has all happened so suddenly. I, who have never been more than a few miles from my home—and now to leave it, to leave my friends, my uncle—"

Malme looked at her keenly. There were no airs about this girl. She was the exact opposite of Vashti, and now Malme doubted that the king, who had found Vashti appealing, would find this unassuming maid to his liking. Naturally, Malme and the eunuchs hoped that the damsel of their choice would be queen.

Presently Sabuchadas came to announce that all was ready.

As Esther, with Malme on one side of her and the two eunuchs following, stepped into the courtyard, an impressive sight awaited them. Soldiers in metal helmets and highly polished cuirasses of metal scales, with gold arm and leg plates and rectangular shields, stood rigidly at attention on either side of three large, curtained litters. Eight half-naked bearers stood at each litter in readiness to lift it upon their brawny shoulders. In the rear was a large wagon for the luggage.

In the first litter, which was the largest and most ornate, Esther was ensconced. The next one, she knew, was for Malme, and the third was for Acratheus and Sabuchadas. Her own litter was almost as large as her bedroom at home. It contained a downy mattress, sumptuously enshrouded in a silken coverlet of pale blue. Many cushions, also covered in silk of blue, pink, lavender and yellow, were so arranged that she could either sit up or recline during the journey. Curtains of heavy green brocade edged with gold and silver embroidery would hide her from the gaze of the curious.

"You are not even to peek out," Sabuchadas ordered as he closed the curtains. "When we are going through a city, you must keep yourself hidden. When we are in the country districts, if you want more air, then you may open the curtains."

She nodded. "I will do as you say," she promised.

Five minutes later she felt the litter being lifted, and knew she was being carried toward one of the gates, followed by the imposing entourage.

Outside the gate the citizens had gathered, disappointed that they were unable to see her. She heard their voices, heard her own name called again and again. Mordecai was in that crowd somewhere, so was the old serving woman and Sarah and Rebecca and various other friends whom perhaps she would never see again. She was glad to be hidden from them, for the tears were coming freely now, tears of excitement and of sorrow at parting from all that was dear and familiar.

Down the long straightness of The Sacred Way went the procession, past the stone lions and the gigantic statues of seated figures. Dogs barked. People shouted, "Esther! Esther! There she goes! She's in that first litter!" The soldiers took out their swords to prevent the press from crowding too close.

When the procession had been on the move for an hour the noise grew less and less. Esther knew that they must be outside the city walls and passing through some suburban district. She was drained of tears now, and she settled among the cushions with bare arms folded beneath her head, trying to imagine what the future held in store for her. Though she found herself wondering how it would feel to be a queen, she had no belief that the king would choose her.

After three hours the procession stopped. The bearers placed the litter gently on the ground, and with large kerchiefs mopped the sweat from their bodies. Acratheus came and opened the curtains. They were outside the city and well off the main highway, near a canal. Because of its ingenious network of many canals, Babylonia was a fertile land. Off in the distance she could see some men digging a trench for another of these irrigation projects. On the right was a wheat field, seemingly stretching on and on to the horizon. On the left was a date grove. Beyond the grove was a wide field of melons ripening in the sun.

The soldiers went off in a group, removing their metal helmets and laying aside their shields. The bearers stretched out on the grass. A fire of coals was being built by men who were evidently cooks, while their assistants took vast quantities of food from various sacks.

Malme brought Esther a basin and towels. The water was fragrantly scented. When she had washed her hands, Sabuchadas brought her a small glass of sesame wine and a plate of fat, juicy grapes.

"We are ordered to proceed with all possible speed," said Malme. "With good weather we should reach Shushan in about eleven days."

"And when we arrive? What then?"

"When all the damsels are assembled, there will be about four hundred of them. Each contestant will be domiciled in what is called The House of the Women."

"Will His Majesty see us all at once?" "No. He will see one each day."

"And if on the first day he finds the one he loves?" Sabuchadas shrugged. "Then the contest is ended, and anyone who so desires may return home with the same escort and courtesy."

An hour later the journey began again. After the sun had set, they stopped. They had reached a governmental post where they would encamp for the night. The empire had a network of fine paved roads and at each day's end was a post for the convenience of those who traveled on official business. For the *angari*, the messengers who went by horseback, there were fresh steeds. For those who traveled by litter there were new bearers. At these posts, fresh food was always waiting.

Malme came, and, closing the curtains, helped Esther change into her night clothes.

"The nights turn cold," said Malme solicitously as she brought a warm wool covering and tucked it about Esther's lithe body. "There, now. Have no fear. You may hear the cries of some wild animal, but there will be guards throughout the night."

As dark descended deeper and deeper, the torches were extinguished and the camp became very still. The soldiers were too exhausted by the long, hot march even to indulge in their favorite pastime of casting lots. Esther lay for a long while, sleepless, staring up at the canopy above her head. She thought of Mordecai, wanting to talk to him, wondering whether he missed her. Through the dark came the bellowing of a herd of wild oxen and the roar of a lion. Knowing herself well guarded, Esther listened to it calmly. Finally she dropped off into a restful, dreamless sleep.

As early as possible next morning, the procession started, so as to take advantage of the coolness. They passed through small towns and cities, but these Esther did not see, for the curtains were closed. Sometimes when the curtains were opened, they passed lonely farm dwellings and people working in the fields, men with cumbersome wooden plows, shepherds tending their flocks, women making butter by vigorously shaking goatskin churns. These isolated ones looked up curiously at the impressive party and then returned to their labors.

Once while passing through a city, Esther heard a commotion to the right of her litter. There were wild screams of agony, and though the bearers did not stop, she unthinkingly opened the curtains sufficiently to peer out. An Amalekite was beating an aged Hebrew wayfarer.

"Dog of a Hebrew! Scum! Filth! How dare you not stand aside as I pass?"

"Sir, I was so loaded with my luggage, I swear I did not see you coming. Ouch! Help! Help!"

But no one ran to help him. People passed quickly with averted eyes. Esther lost all pleasure in traveling now. As the frantic cries of the Israelite receded in the distance, she lay back, sick, confused, quivering. Oh, that she could do some thing to help her people! She recalled how unruffled the passersby had been by the scene, as though they were accustomed to such things. She remembered the blood gushing from the man's mouth. She heard again his pitiable cries for help. She recalled the loathing in the eyes of the Amalekite. One race held in abject terror by the other. She lay with her face down, weeping for a long time. Such a thing might happen someday to Uncle Mordecai and she would not be there to bind up his wounds.

When they stopped that night and Malme came to open the curtains, Esther was no longer in tears, but Malme remarked that she looked tired.

"It is not tiredness," confessed Esther miserably. "I saw the Amalekite beating that Hebrew. It is horrible. And no one helped. No one did anything."

Malme shrugged. "Because we have an Amalekite for prime minister, the Amalekites are everywhere in power. It is a shame, but nothing can be done about it. The Hebrews do not harm anyone. They mind their own business. In Shushan they have a large quarter and they never leave it unless they have to."

"This Haman, the prime minister, is he truly so close to the king as they say?"

"So close that His Majesty calls him father, and trusts him implicitly. I say no more, for I do not criticize my king."

Night came, the eighth night of their journey, and the camp settled down to slumber. To Esther it seemed that awaiting her in Shushan were evil forces, mute, stealthy and menacing. Shushan seemed remote, but the evil forces seemed close.

5: The House of the Women

BABYLON was old and beautiful, treasuring the glories of her past, renewing her old buildings reverently as though they were shrines. Shushan, though even more populous, prided herself upon being modern. To Shushan carne the world's most renowned designers, architects, sculptors and craftsmen. Teeming Shushan, progressive and stimulating, drew the great ones like a magnet from all parts of the earth.

The city had an architecture peculiar to herself, a mixture which tastefully incorporated the best of every nation, yet managed somehow to retain a style distinctly Persian. All the buildings looked new. Even the hordes of well-dressed people on the streets had a vigor, a style, and a pride that was not seen in Babylon. The very air was fresh and spicy.

Overlooking the city was the palace, a veritable citadel, rising terrace upon terrace above its own stout walls. 'Esther could not resist peeping from her curtains when they reached the enormous main entrance to the palace grounds. Here was a wide paved court where many people were standing, but many others were coming and going, some in litters, some on horseback, others walking.

Bounded by its high walls, the palace area stretched miles upon miles, a glorious city within a city. In the midst of it, fronting the courtyard, was the king's palace. No one could mistake it—a place of alabaster. Surely, thought Esther, this was paradise on earth.

On entering the gate, the soldiers dispersed. They had fulfilled their mission. The three litters were carried along a winding path which circled to the left of the king's palace. Finally the bearers stopped, laid Esther's litter gently to the ground, and almost as they did so, Acratheus and Sabuchadas were opening the curtains.

"We are here, lady," said Sabuchadas. "Welcome to Shushan."

She stepped from the shelter of the litter and stood gazing about with the appreciative eyes of a child suddenly transported into fairyland. The air was heavy with the fragrance of countless flowers. It pulsed with the song of birds. A soft, fresh breeze touched her cheeks and throat. The thought came to her, "Oh, if Uncle Mordecai could only see this!"

"Come," said Acratheus.

He led her toward the door of a large house, Malme and Sabuchadas following. At their approach the door was opened by another eunuch, obviously a door tender. Malme had already explained that all the attendants would be either women or eunuchs.

At a table on which was a large ledger, sat another eunuch, who, Esther surmised, was the custodian of this particular house. Acratheus addressed him respectfully.

"Greetings, Hegai."

"Greetings."

Hegai scarcely raised his eyes from the ledger. So many beautiful girls had passed through that door lately that he was bored. Some put on commanding airs as though they were already queen, others looked at him brazenly as if to say, "Here I am. Admire me." Others simpered at him, as if saying to themselves, "Here is someone in authority. I will try to get on the right side of him. He will make things easy for me."

And some were so frightened that he could almost hear the throbbing of their hearts. Others began blabbing at once that the journey had been hot and tiresome. Others were merely uneasy, and betrayed their uneasiness by continuously fussing with their neck chains or bracelets.

"We bring the entry from the city of Babylon," said Acratheus.

"Her name?" "Esther."

"Her age?"

"Seventeen."

Now for the first time Hegai looked up at "the entry from Babylon." She smiled, and it was the smile of one friend meeting another friend. Esther's smile was so radiant, so infectious, so charming, and above all so friendly, that it was impossible even for one as hardened as Hegai not to smile back at her.

His eyes met those of Acratheus. "I will send the seven maidens for attendance. You will escort her to the apartment in the front at the left."

"And when shall we accomplish her preparation for meeting His Majesty?"

"It has been decided that each damsel shall have her audience with the king in the order of her arrival. There are sixty more to come. Your lady is number three-forty."

"So be it. Come then, Esther."

Her companions led her down a long marble corridor with a high vaulted ceiling and a mosaic floor which must have been freshly scrubbed, for not a sandal mark showed on it. Everything was spacious, everything was neat, and so quiet was this house that one would never suspect that three hundred and forty girls, each with ten attendants, were already in residence here.

The newcomers mounted a wide marble stairway. On the second floor Acratheus, muttering that he could hardly wait to get something to eat, led the way along another corridor where every door was closed.

"The three hundred and fortieth," Malme fumed. "What chance will she have after he has seen three hundred and thirty-nine ahead of her?"

The room they entered was large and luxurious. It was not a single room, but rather a suite of four rooms, each having doors leading into the main room. The door at the right opened into a dormitory, tidy and simple, where the seven maidservants would sleep. There were two doors at the left. One led to a room which was commodious and elaborate, and which would accommodate Acratheus and Sabuchadas. The smaller room, no less tastefully and richly furnished, was for Malme. The largest and most elegant of all was Esther's. .

She stood entranced in the middle of it. There was a large bed, big enough for three people, with a silver-brocade coverlet. The bedstead was of carved ivory, a creation of such exquisitely delicate workmanship that it appeared to be made of lace. Tall windows, heavily curtained, faced the south. Despite the heaviness of the curtains, they were so woven that the room was flooded with sunlight.

"Does every damsel have accommodations like this?" Esther asked in a tone of frank astonishment.

"Yes," replied Sabuchadas, "although this is the best. This place is called The House of the Women. It is used by female visitors—wives and daughters of visiting potentates. Near by is a second House of the Women, but this is the better of the two. Every establishment on the king's premises has its own staff and is in charge of one person. Hegai is in command here."

"Now you must know the rules of this place," said Acratheus sternly. "Your meals will be served here. It is forbidden to visit from room to room. Damsels will not be permitted to form friendships with fellow-contestants. This is because we who are in charge of each maiden hope that our lady will be queen. It is for us to design her clothes, oversee her food, choose what jewels and perfumes she will use. We do not want this divulged, since if it is good it might be copied. Now, at the rear of this house is a walled court. Here, twice a day, the entrants will walk for air and exercise. This will be your only contact with the others, and you are not permitted to leave this house until after your interview with the king."

"I am not even to see the palace grounds?" asked Esther in a tone of disappointment,

"They are so large," answered Malme evasively. "It would take days and days to cover all the territory enclosed within the royal walls."

"But not any of it?"

Sensing the keenness of her disappointment, the three gazed at one another inquiringly.

"We-ell," said Malme at last, as though humoring a child, "it is not permitted, and we and Hegai would be taking a great risk, but—perhaps a short tour at once—"

"Oh, could we?"

"You're not tired from the journey?"

"Tired! Oh, no!" Esther wondered how they could think she was tired when she had spent the entire journey reclining.

"Well, I will ask Hegai," said Malme, and hurried out.

No sooner had she gone than the seven maids arrived. These girls were between the ages of sixteen and twenty-five. They had been trained to move quietly and not to speak unless it was necessary.

Esther listened while Acratheus outlined her duties to each maid. One was merely to make the bed and see that no dust accumulated in the carving. Another was to serve the lady's meals. The third was to attend to her baths and shampoos. The fourth was to clean her room. The fifth was to clean the other rooms. The sixth and seventh were to wield the large fans, so as to keep the room cool and without flies.

By the time Acratheus had finished, Malme was back. "He says that if she goes at once, and heavily veiled, she may spend three hours seeing the sights within the palace walls."

"So be it," said Acratheus. "Sabuchadas, you be her guide. I am famishing."

Esther put on her veil and, heart thumping with excitement, followed Sabuchadas outside.

"Will we see the king?" she asked eagerly.

"Oh, no. When his Majesty is not in council, he sits all day hearing cases which the judges cannot decide. Any male citizen, if he desires, may declare at his trial, 'I appeal to the king.' He is usually sorry afterward, for this means that he will have to report in the outer court each day, waiting in the vestibule for months until his turn comes. This is a court day and His Majesty will be engaged from sunup to well after sundown."

Her guide pointed out the immense vestibule, or outer court, through which her procession had entered. It was open to the sky, and paved with colored marble. This was the place where the people waited to be called before the king. Beyond this was the inner court.

He told her that the throne room was designed like a Greek temple and covered two and a half acres. This, he explained, they could not enter, but they were in the palace itself now, and he showed her the banquet room and the trophy room.

"Only the king and his personal servants live in the king's palace. This is as much as I can show you of it, and if you linger, staring at everything like this, you will see nothing in three hours."

So they left the palace by a side entrance. From this vantage point, what an expanse of beauty lay stretched before them! Here were porticoes, colonnades and staircases, opening onto a terrace which Sabuchadas said covered forty-five acres. This acreage was divided in two parts by a pylon. On the left was a vast level space which was the parade ground, where the king reviewed his troops and where infantry and cavalry drilled. Beyond this was the arsenal, the officers' quarters, and the building which housed the enlisted men.

Now Sabuchadas directed Esther's gaze to the other side of the pylon, and she gave an involuntary exclamation of delight, for here was a building of multi-colored enamels. On the top of it was a hanging garden, and the structure was surrounded by a grove of pistachio and other nut trees.

Oh, she thought ecstatically, if only Uncle Mordecai were here!

Next, Sabuchadas showed her the stables for the king's horses—a structure of white marble with mangers of highly burnished gold. Then came the king's carriage house, where there were chariots and litters of many sizes and styles. Near this was a building which housed the king's animals—elephants, camels, monkeys, hunting dogs, and cats with staring, saucer-round eyes and long silky hair. Next came the king's own tabernacle with a court paved with colored marbles. Near it was the priests' house. Each edifice was set at least an acre from the other, yet all were connected in one flawlessly landscaped whole by winding paths and luxuriant, scrupulously kept gardens.

"And this," said Sabuchadas, "is the queen's palace."

It was an alabaster structure, a companion to the king's 'palace, but slightly smaller. It had many windows, but each was curtained so that no one could see in. Like every other building in Shushan, it was of Persian architecture, yet combining the best features of Babylon, Egypt and Greece.

After three hours Esther and Sabuchadas returned to The House of the Women. Hegai was still seated in his place by the door, and tossing back her veil Esther smiled at him. "Oh, sir, it was wonderful!"

He smiled, too. "In three scant hours you could not have seen one tenth of it. Tell no one that you've had this experience. It would go hard with me if it were known." He looked at Sabuchadas. "The one from Ecbatana in Media has just arrived. If she is the best that city can do—" He sighed. "Fifty-nine more to come. Truly, I tell you, I would this were over!"

Esther really was tired now. She and her companion had walked at least four miles, but it was impossible to lie down, for reaching her own room she found Malme and Acratheus already surrounded by samples of various fabrics. Esther must have her sandal size taken, her ring size taken, her measurements taken. She must have her hair washed and her nails manicured, and when the long day ended she like Hegai began to wish that this whole thing were over.

Weary as she was, she lay sleepless on her magnificent ivory bed, thinking of all the sights she had seen, thinking of Mordecai, but most of all, thinking that not far away was the king, the man for whose delight all this splendor had been created.

Every afternoon following the midday meal four hundred girls left their rooms to stroll about the court—a place of trees, benches, winding walks and gardens.

Here were country girls, not always beautiful, but the first choice of their districts. Here were sophisticated city girls, accustomed to opulence, pampered darlings out of castles.

Between these times in the open, the girls were kept busy by perfumers, weavers, dyers and jewellers who came to inspect them and to create just the right perfumes, dye the colors, weave the fabrics which would offset the individuality and beauty of each contestant. Special food was prepared, not only that their breath should remain sweet, but that those who were too thin would gain weight and those too plump would lose it.

Instructors taught them to walk, stand, bow, kneel. Physicians came to examine them.

Malme, Acratheus and Sabuchadas were in charge of Esther.

They had to approve everything before she ate it, used it or wore it. They experimented with various coiffures and headdresses. Every style robe was tried and many styles abandoned. The length and set of a veil, the mere tying of a scarf, required lengthy consultation. The width of a girdle, the fullness of a cape and its proper draping—nothing was overlooked.

Finally the day came when each girl's mentors reported to Hegai that their charge was ready.

The day the first girl went to the king, all the others were excited, eagerly awaiting her return in order to ask such questions as, "What does he look like? What did he say? How tall is he? How did he act?" But when a girl left The House of the Women she did not return to it.

It became easy to recognize those whose turns were near.

Some flew into tantrums with their servants. Some paced madly along the paths. Others would sit on a bench staring wretchedly into space.

"It is my turn next," whispered a Median, as Esther was standing under a pomegranate tree one evening. "What shall I say to him?"

Since Esther could not answer that question, she countered with another. "Tell me, what is your number?"

"I shall be the hundredth he has seen."

She was a small girl with vivacious dark eyes, a brown skin and a bold mouth. Heretofore she had had an imperious air, walking with her head high and a stretched-up torso. But now she was diffident and pale.

Next night, when Malme brought Esther a dish of dates, she asked if the king had chosen the Median. Malme said no.

"I cannot understand it, Malme. Surely, ninety out of the hundred girls he has seen are beautiful. What is he looking for in a woman?"

Malme did not know.

In The House of the Women Esther passed her eighteenth birthday, for now she had been there over a year.

As the day for her meeting with the king grew nearer, Malme grew tense. Acratheus and Sabuchadas grew more taciturn.

Esther smiled at them. "If so far the king has seen no one who pleases him, surely he'll not be pleased with me. That girl from Thrace was dazzling. The one from Sardis was regal. The one from Memphis was especially lovely, so was the one from Thebes. As for me, I never expected my turn would come. I never really expected to be chosen."

"Nonsense. You are the loveliest of all."

"You think so because you're fond of me. Poor Malme! After all the trouble you have taken with me, it is you who will be disappointed. You have told me all there is to know about perfumes, cosmetics, jewels, deportment, clothes. But why do not you advise me how to act with this stranger when I am presented to him?"

Malme's eyes took on a baffled, helpless look. "Because I do not know. Some men like a froward girl and some are attracted to one who is shy and reserved. There is no telling about men. Wise though the king is, he was ensnared by that she-devil, Vashti." For a time Malme fell silent. "Do you fear him?" she asked at length.

"Yes, I fear him. He is so wonderful. He is so great. I shall not know what to say to him. He will find me stupid. He will be bored." After a time she asked, "Malme, will he kiss me?"

"How do I know?" asked Malme fretfully. She looked old and tired. These months had been a strain.

Some days later Acratheus told Esther about the laws of Persia, how, for instance, it was forbidden under pain of death for anyone, even the queen, to approach the king without his permission. However, if anyone did so, and the king reached his scepter toward the person, it meant the person was pardoned. Esther listened attentively, and when the lesson in law ended, she went into the court. It now seemed almost empty, for less than a hundred girls remained.

She did not stroll along the paths that day, but sat on a bench staring dismally at the treetops. Suppose the king should be ugly, gross, ill mannered, shattering all her dreams of him? She almost wished she might catch some disease so that she would have an excuse to avoid the meeting.

A girl came and sat beside her, a girl with a slim body and brazen blue eyes and a slightly flushed face.

"It is my turn tomorrow," announced the girl happily.

"And you are not afraid?"

"Not at all. I shall make him love me. I am a Chaldean. I shall carry a love charm. It cannot fail."

"You are tall and you look like a queen."

"I had my stars read when I was little. They proclaimed high honors for me. I believe in the stars. The stars do not lie."

The two girls did not speak again, and presently Hegai summoned them all inside.

Next day Esther asked Malme if the king had chosen the Chaldean.

"No. Your time comes closer."

Esther felt suddenly remote from Malme. Would her time come at all? She walked to the window and stared out upon this paradise. It was love she wanted—not homage, not position, not wealth. Love. She thought how sweet it would be to be beloved. It did not matter that he was king. Love mattered. She wanted to love the man she married. She wanted him to love her—utterly, devotedly. And did a king want love, too, just simple love? Or did he want a woman who was clever, worldly-wise and scintillating, who was beautiful so that he could be proud to show her to his guests? What did a king want? For what was he seeking? All this while he had rarely been absent from her thought. She turned away from the window, her eyes somber. Everything about her was so quiet that she could hear the beating of her heart.

Malme noted that dreaming, brooding look in her eyes, and thought how calm she was. "I am more impatient than she," Malme murmured.

Days passed with unbearable slowness now. The wardrobe had been chosen. The beauty culture had become routine. The three mentors and the seven maids moved about the room pursuing their duties with a kind of fervent urgency which increased as the time grew nearer.

At last it was a week before Esther's turn. That was the day when an Amalekite girl went to the palace. The girl was sure she would be chosen, for wasn't the prime minister one of her race? She laughed coyly, showing strong white teeth that flashed enticingly against the vivid red of her painted lips. Was not the king partial to Amalekites?

The Amalekite stood, leaning against the trunk of an olive tree, smiling. She had the lean, sharp face of the Amalekites, with thin nostrils and long upper lip. There was a wildness, a recklessness about her. Her bold dark eyes were pert and bright.

Esther regarded her gravely. "Yes," she admitted. "I think he will choose you. There is something flashing about you, something exhilarating in the way you walk."

Before the Amalekite could answer, two of her attendants summoned her inside and she walked jauntily into the house.

But the next day another girl left for the palace.

And finally Esther awoke one morning filled with the awareness that tomorrow was her turn. Wildly, she wished herself back in Babylon.

I do not want the crown unless love comes with it, she thought firmly.

As the day progressed Esther's mood changed to one of indifference, and she said to herself, "Let it be as God wills."

That afternoon Acratheus and Sabuchadas inspected anew her presentation robe, laid out the jewels and sandals she was to wear next day. The bulging eyes of Acratheus looked dull, as if already the long strain was over and he had resigned himself to Esther's dismissal.

"We have done our best," said Sabuchadas. "Now we can only wait."

Malme went out and presently returned with an armful of flowers. "We are too glum," she muttered as she arranged them in vases. "They may add cheer to this room."

"Oh, how beautiful!" exclaimed Esther. "Truly, I have never seen such flowers!"

"It has taken a great deal of care to bring them to such beauty," replied Malme. "Flowers are like women. They need to be cared for."

Esther turned away from the flowers and sighed. "If I fail to appeal to the king—"

"Then either we shall take you back to your uncle or you will enter the second House of the Women under the custody of one named Shaashgaz," replied Acratheus. "And you will probably never see us again. Now, we must not any of us feel bad about this. We must accept whatever happens, accept it without complaint, as the tamarisk tree accepts both sun and rain, as the forest accepts both sunrise and moonlight. But—I wish tomorrow were over!"

6: Ahasuerus

HOPING to put the aspirants at ease, Ahasuerus did not receive them in the throne room. He sat at the far end of an incredibly long room with tall windows through which the sunlight fell in oblong patterns upon the stone floor. This room was reserved for private discussions. It lacked the cathedral-like aspect of the throne room, being somewhat gay with its white and blue hangings fastened by silver chains to marble pillars.

At these meetings he did not wear his crown, but wore instead the kingly *kidarion*, or embroidered turban. His robe combined the royal hues of purple, deep blue and crimson. In his hand he held the scepter, without which the king of the Medes and Persians could never be seen.

The chair upon which he sat was elevated from the floor by a wide dais with thick Persian rugs. It was canopied with silk dyed in the royal colors—blue and purple. He was alone in the stillness, alone and bored and weary. For over a year now, in addition to the countless affairs of state which pressed upon him demanding attention, he had been compelled to give precious hours to this business of finding a queen. Each day through that door facing him at the opposite end of the room had come a different girl.

Some were so beset with shyness that they were rigid. Their smiles were stiff and painful and they stammered when they spoke. Some, afraid of saying the wrong things, had been mute. Others had swaggered as they approached him, with swaying hips and bold eyes and practiced, insincere smiles. Some had been clever and loquacious, seeking acceptance through their scintillating wit and sophistication. Others sought to entice him by slyly touching his sinewy arm, by coyness and flattery. Still others had assumed an air of hauteur which they thought he would require in a queen.

Some he had hated and some he had pitied, some had amused him and some he had admired, but each had lacked the essential spark which would find a response in him. He could not define what it was. He had treated them all in a courtly way, yet unable to mask completely the estrangement he had felt.

He could not terminate these audiences, since he had agreed to them, and a king's word, especially the word of a Persian, could not be broken. He understood that there were some fifty more girls with whom he must dine and converse while important matters waited.

The noise and bustle of the outer court could not reach him here, but he knew a multitude of people were waiting to see him, longing for decisions upon their problems, and he must sit and talk to some strange and perhaps simpering girl of inconsequential things! What a waste of valuable time! Fifty more days of this. Fifty more days of sheer boredom.

The door at the far end of the room opened. The voice of Hegai rang through the stillness in full, throaty tones.

"Behold Esther of Babylon!"

Then the door closed and there was only this slender figure in white moving along the expanse of floor. As yet she was too far from him to distinguish her features, but he was struck by the grace with which she moved.

This one, at least, had poise, exquisite poise. She did not hurry toward him as some had done, nor did she gaze about the room in awe. Lightly, effortlessly, she kept coming forward, moving from shadow into sunlight as she passed the many windows.

Several feet from the dais she sank to her knees with the usual greeting.

"O King, live forever!"

"Rise, Esther." She rose. "Come closer." She walked toward him, her gaze artless and bright, unwavering yet without boldness.

She thought, "This is he! This is the king! Oh, how tired he is, how tired and unhappy. Poor man, so tired! Not a great king, really, only tired. And oh, how handsome he is!" She forgot herself completely in genuine admiration and consideration for this man.

"Speak, Esther. Let me hear your voice again. Come, do not be frightened. Sit here, facing me." He motioned to a chair near him on the dais.

"Your Majesty—" her voice was low, compassionate, soothing, magnetic. There was in it something he had never known before, something maternal and tender. "Your Majesty, if only by some magic I could relieve this deep, deep tiredness in you!"

He was startled. Here was a girl who was thinking, not of herself and the impression she was making, but of him! And how had she known he was tired, not having slept last night because of work which could not be put aside?

"You are—wondrous sweet," he said. "This concern for me is unusual and it has a ring of sincerity. You are comfortable in that chair?"

"Quite."

In a long, probing gaze, their eyes met.

"Is the damsel from Babylon afraid of me?" he asked at length.

She smiled. "No, my king, not now. But sometimes when I contemplated this interview, I was filled with terror, quite convinced that I should stumble on my way to you!"

He laughed—and it was a long time since he had laughed; yet the way she said it, with that charming, artless little gesture of her hand and the humorous lifting at the corners of her enticing mouth—and now as he looked more closely at it, it was an enticing mouth, not heavily painted as had been some of the others, but revealing all the delectable softness of its natural contours—a mouth neither too thin nor too wide, too long nor too short, just right.

"I suppose," he said, a certain coldness creeping into his voice, "you would like to be queen?"

The smile had gone from her eyes now. They were clear eyes, honest eyes, and she spoke simply. "In truth, Your Majesty, I would not have dreamed so high. And when it seemed that my turn would really come, then I began to ponder that question seriously; and I knew quite surely that— "

"Well?"

"That I would not want to wear the crown unless I could love with all my heart the one who placed it on my head. Love is more important to a woman, I think, than all the rest. Though she live in a palace, she is poor who has it not. Whether he be king or commoner, I want to love my husband, and—I want to be sure—oh, *sure* that he loves me!"

"Humph," he said.

She thought that she had displeased him, yet she was glad she had spoken freely. Indeed, she had not expected to feel so at ease with him.

"I am Your Majesty's loyal subject," she continued, undisturbed by his silence, "and I would be content to go on, being nothing more. But your frank question, do I want to be queen, demands a frank answer, and now I say—No, Your Highness. I do not wish to be queen unless the crown includes the heart."

She spoke without affectation, simply and sincerely. It was utterly impossible for him to doubt her sincerity. Sincerity. How rare it was! He sat, chin in hand, regarding her, and it came to him during that time of silence that health, honesty, sincerity, tenderness, sweetness, wisdom, compassion, poise and charm, *these* were the things which comprised true beauty in a woman. These were attributes which adorned a woman as no jewels could. And he knew instinctively that these priceless qualities were possessed by this girl, this stranger, who, in some miraculous way, was not a stranger at all, but rather seemed to be someone whom he had always known.

Was she more beautiful than the others? He did not know. Perhaps her loveliness consisted of this inner beauty which radiated through her. He felt its warmth. He was no longer tired, no longer concerned with the tasks awaiting him, no longer oppressed by them.

And Esther, sitting beside him, felt relaxed and at ease. His thoughtful silence, his keen, dark eyes, produced no element of apprehension in her. This was her king. This was the man whose profile she had seen on coins. As he studied her, she studied him, delighting in the clear-cut features, the strong, firm mouth, the aristocratic nose, the dark, heavily lidded eyes and the clean, level sweep of his brows. She admired the patrician straightness of his forehead, the full, curling hair, and now, oddly, she found herself longing to touch his hair, to smooth it tenderly. Her eyes dropped to the hand which rested on the arm of his chair, the hand that held the scepter.

As if he felt her thoughts, he put the scepter aside. "Now there is no longer a king in this room."

"There are only two friends," she answered softly.

"Friends! How few true friends I have! Truly, a friend is more precious than rubies." He leaned back in the tall chair, a smile of amusement tugging at the corners of his mouth. "So! You have come to the conclusion that life owes you, not a kingdom, but love?" The mouth lost its hint of a smile and became bitter. "Love! I have never known what real love is. In truth, I have been too busy to think much about it."

It was pleasant just to look at this girl. From moment to moment her beauty increased. His hand reached out and touched hers. She blushed, inwardly stirred at the touch. She did not move her hand away, but let it rest, small and yielding, beneath his. As he continued speaking, talking now of his hope for peace and of his desire for more trading ships, she said to herself that it was wonderful to sit with him and be his confidante.

"I love this man," she told herself. "Yes! I love him even more than Mordecai. I love him. I love him. I love him."

A knock upon the side door, and the king took his hand away to grasp the scepter. At his command to enter, Bigthan opened the door and bowed low.

"If it please the king, it is time for the midday meal. Will the king be served?"

"Yes. Here."

Bigthan withdrew. A few minutes later a table was brought and placed in the middle of the room. Then Bigthan and Teresh, accompanied by five other servants, arrived with the food.

Ahasuerus offered Esther his hand and led her to the table.

A servant poured cool, scented water over their hands and gave them napkins of fine Egyptian linen.

The king ate heartily, but Esther, filled with the wonder of new love, had no interest in food. When the meal was over,

Ahasuerus suggested a stroll through his private gardens. They walked along the paths under the trees, and finally they found a bench which faced a large pool where, beneath the surface, one caught the swift flash of darting goldfish. The birds sang zestfully, looking with bright eyes and tiny, sidewise heads, upon this young couple who seemed to have so much to talk about.

The afternoon passed and the two on the bench were unmindful of time, until Ahasuerus noted that the sun's rays were slanting into his eyes. He did not want this day to end. He did not want to let this girl go.

"Do you have parents, brothers, sisters?" he asked.

"No, Your Majesty. I am an orphan. I have no living relative except an uncle who brought me up."

"I, too, am an orphan and without close relatives. Have they told you, Esther, what it would mean to be the wife of a king?"

"We have not discussed such things, Your Majesty."

"You would live in yonder palace. You will see only women and eunuchs, unless I consent. That is the law. In Persia, we hold the law to be a sacred thing. You could not even approach me unless I summoned you. That, too, is a law. I would rarely have time to visit you, perhaps only once a month because often I labor with my scribes until daybreak. But you will have unlimited power and unlimited wealth. You rule in your own palace. You can change its furnishings as you like. You—" he paused at the startled expression in her eyes. "What is it, Esther?"

"Why, it is only—I was thinking, my lord, that—that you speak as though—as though it were all— all settled!"

Her words took him sharply aback. Their eyes met. The sun was red now, its splendor illuminating both young faces. And soul spoke silently to soul, unveiling the glory of love, and in love's wondrous glow the whole earth seemed permeated with that glory. In that flash he knew that love had come, the love he had missed in his life of strain and pressure, and this love was a thing so powerful that it could lift him above mundane matters, making him so free that he seemed weightless. Love. Here it was, shining out unmasked from their faces. How long they stood there, looking at each other in that charged silence, neither knew.

"Settled?" he said at last. "But certainly, it is settled! I want no woman but you!" He rose. Gripping her arms above the elbows, he lifted her to her feet. Then he took her in his arms.

"You want love? I will give you the love of my heart and life! And now I know that I am incapable of a puny, lukewarm love. No. I pledge you my heart's devotion. I love you. I never thought to love like this. Love is the worker of miracles. Never have I felt so happy, so free from care. Has love done that to me, Esther? Can love work such magic as this? Can love come so suddenly?"

She clung to him, her eyes wet with tears. Now at last her hands reached up and smoothed the black curls as she had longed to do for hours. "Oh, in my arms you will find peace and rest from all that troubles you! May I please you in all ways! May I never bring you one moment of grief or pain! Truly, truly, I am rich in love! I have loved you since I was a little girl. I will love you as long as I live!" She laughed excitedly softly. "And I wondered what I would say to you! Why, my heart spoke—and yours answered!"

He kissed her, a long, sweet kiss. When at last they drew apart, he laughed like a boy—and kissed her again. Then he said only one word.

"Come!"

Holding her by the hand, he led her back to the palace, this time into the throne room. Straight up to the elevation of the throne they went, and with his golden scepter he touched a gong. Scarcely had it ceased reverberating than Teresh opened the door and bowed.

"Your Majesty wishes?"

"Summon the councillors and the household and all who are at this moment within my gates!"

"Your Majesty," asked Esther when the servant had gone "what are you going to do?"

"I am going to announce to all 'the world that my search is ended and that I have found the damsel most pleasing to me in the length and breadth of my kingdom. Come, beloved, do not tremble so. Take your place here beside me, facing them. It is your *rightful* place, always—always by my side. When the announcement has been made, you will go at once to the queen's palace. I will not see you again until our wedding day. Feel free there to make what changes are pleasing to you, buy anything your heart desires."

She was not trembling now. She could feel his love about her, warm and protective, giving her strength and support to face a multitude. And a multitude it was. They came in softly, and they kept coming until the huge room was packed. Hundreds of faces. Myriad colors. She saw Malme, Acratheus, Sabuchadas and Hegai, looking very proud. She saw the councillors in their robes of state, and at the front of the crowd she saw the man whom she knew to be Haman, the Amalekite.

Confronting all these people, the king's stature seemed to increase. He was a tall man, but now he appeared even taller. His voice carried to every part of the long room. There was joy in it, such joy as they had never heard from him.

"Be it known to you that my choice is made!"

There was a murmur of approval. There were nods and smiles and heads bobbing, as if they all shared in this dynamic moment. Haman smiled, too, but it was a smileless smile that inched its way slowly along the brown, thin, Amalekite face with its high nose and sharp, beady eyes and colorless slit of a mouth. He is old and sly, thought Esther. She felt his eyes and inwardly recoiled, as though she had been touched by a rat.

"I have chosen," went on Ahasuerus, "a damsel out of Babylon. I shall marry her and make her my lawful wife, your queen. Hail Queen Esther!"

"Hail Queen Esther!" echoed heartily from over a thousand throats.

"We will have the wedding on the twelfth of Adar. As you know, this is the seventh year of my reign. I decree that *angari* be sent throughout my empire and unto every nation. I give orders for a national holiday, that all peoples may keep a feast of my wedding. It will be known as 'Esther's Feast.' I, myself, for a full month, will give a feast to all Persians and Medes, to the rulers of every nation and to my worthy friends and councillors. Hail Queen Esther!"

"Hail Queen Esther! Hail Queen Esther!"

He waved his scepter with an imperious gesture of dismissal. Esther stood, straight and slim, thinking how swiftly the *angari* would reach Babylon and how, after a blare of trumpets, the news would be announced. And Mordecai would hear it. And for a full month all Babylon would hold festival.

Mordecai. How would he feel? The queen's uncle. The rabbis and her people in the Hebrew section would pray for her. Before coming to this meeting with the king, she had prayed that God's will, and only His will, be done, and now she felt that this was His will that she, who was of royal blood, should wear a crown.

When the room was silent again and the door was closed, he turned to her. "My queen, my love! You stand even now at the throne. And how do you like it?"

"You are standing with me, you love me, and so I am happy. Oh, I am wondrously happy!"

"And I. I want to share my joy with all the world. You will never lie to me, I feel that. You will never fail me, will you? Let me look into your eyes again. Yes, candor is there, and feeling, and truth. These are priceless. *This* is the beauty that I see in you—the inner beauty, shining through!"

7: The Coronation

MALME, Sabuchadas and Acratheus were waiting outside the door when the king escorted Esther to it and put her in their charge with a short speech which commended them for their care of "Her Majesty" and promised them liberal rewards for their faithfulness. Then he left, proceeding toward the council chamber.

Malme, Acratheus and Sabuchadas bowed low before Esther. Being bowed down to, being spoken of as "Her Majesty" produced a reaction of discomfort, but Esther told herself that she must accept all this as rightfully hers and in a short time she would grow accustomed to it.

She flashed her charming smile at them and spoke with her natural simplicity. "Good friends, rejoice in my happiness! I'm supremely happy. And I'm grateful to you three. This exalted position to which the king has elevated me is filled with hazards. I want—oh, with all my heart I want to be a good wife and a good queen! Now more than ever I need your help and loyalty."

"We are grateful," replied Acratheus, "that Your Majesty finds us to her liking still, after this difficult year through which we have passed together. But that is ended now. This day a new adventure begins! May Esther's reign be glorious!"

Without waiting for her reply, he put the veil over her face, turned, and led the way, not back to The House of the Women, but along the path to the queen's palace.

They entered into a great hall almost as large as the throne room. Here the staff of servants had already assembled. All of them dropped to their knees at Esther's entrance. Except for the seven maids who had been in attendance upon her, every face was strange. There must, she thought, have been over a hundred people—cooks, gardeners, cleaners. She did not know what to say to them.

But the capable Acratheus relieved her of all embarrassment.

When the general obeisance was over, he waved them away with a lordly gesture of his fat, ringed hand. Then he turned to his mistress.

"What is Your Majesty's wish?"

She gazed about her. This palace had been Vashti's, but it would be her future home. The thought came to her that she wanted no trace to remain of the former queen, nothing to remind Ahasuerus of a pain that was past. Besides, this hall was too crowded, the colors were too harsh, and the arrangement of the furnishings was not artistic.

"There are changes I would make, and I wish them made at once. Acratheus, you will be custodian. You will attend to the entire workings of this house. Sabuchadas, you will be his assistant."

"I am honored at this promotion," said Acratheus. "I will serve you faithfully until I die."

She touched his arm lightly. "I know that. And Malme, you will be my chief maid—and my friend."

Malme choked. "I have prayed that it might be so!"

"And now we shall look over the house."

It was growing dark, and they proceeded by lamplight through the rooms.

On the main floor, in addition to the enormous reception hall, was a banquet room capable of seating a thousand guests. Beyond this was a large serving room which was connected with the kitchen. Then there was a smaller room where the queen dined alone with the king or a few friends. There was an office, reception room, bedroom and dining room for the custodian, which would now belong to Acratheus. There was the formal "queen's audience room" with its dais and throne. On the second floor was the queen's apartment with a bed of solid, intricately carved gold, and a floor inlaid with red, blue and black marble. Off this was the queen's dressing room and a parlor where she would receive her close friends. The rest of the house contained storerooms and rooms for the servants.

In the rooms of state and her own apartment, Esther wanted softer, more restful colors. She discarded some of the furniture and with infallible taste commanded a more harmonious arrangement of that which she retained; but even this she wanted upholstered in different shades.

The house, near the king's, was connected with his by means of the courtyard, which had a door through which only he could enter. Like his palace, this house was set upon a knoll so that it overlooked even the boundary walls, and from her bed-chamber on the second floor, she could see one entire side of the city. From another window she could see the public court.

The queen's private courtyard was enclosed in high walls, insuring absolute privacy, and since everything here was conceived on a stupendous scale, this court covered an area of three acres. It was skillfully landscaped, every path leading outward from a large fountain and pool. Each path was shaded by blossoming trees so that the queen could walk where she would without danger of having her fair skin marred by the sun.

Alone in her room at last, Esther thought back over this long and memorable day. She remembered being dressed in her white robe and how Malme's usually steady hands had trembled. She recalled the critical gaze of Acratheus as he subjected her to a final inspection. She remembered one of the maids placing before her a light breakfast of milk, rice, fruit and nuts, and when she could not eat, the three had seemed to understand.

She remembered Ahasuerus, every word he had said to her, living over their meeting, and even recalling certain little things which she had not consciously noticed at the time. The slanting light of the sun on the fish pool. The peacefulness of the king's garden. A thousand things pressed forward into her mind, as though demanding to be remembered and relived.

Her future was settled. And yet—was it? She remembered Vashti, and shuddered. Perhaps Vashti had thought, too, "My future is settled" the first night *she* had stayed in this room.

A mistake, the breaking of a law, and though Ahasuerus might love her, she would share Vashti's fate. Yes, henceforth she must tread warily, weighing every word and act.

And now, along the paved highways, racing in all directions on their fast horses, stopping at the posthouses only long enough to mount fresh steeds, went the *angari*. On they went, on and on, announcing that Persia was soon to have a new queen—a damsel named Esther.

The generous, vigorous Persians would drink her health and poets would compose lyrics to extol her. Suddenly, people in the hilltops and people in the valleys would be aware of a new name—Esther. Those who lived in palaces would hear it, and those who lived in solitude. And from now on rich women and poor would choose the colors favored by this hitherto unknown girl.

Sheep and kids would be killed in preparation for "Esther's Feast." In the temples of every sect, prayers would be said for her. She recalled those high temple towers in Babylon with the image of the god at the top, reached by an exterior staircase. Little did she dream as she passed those places with Mordecai on their sight-seeing tours that one day people would mount those stairs to pray for her.

Her heart quickened as she thought of Ahasuerus, and she tried to judge him impartially. Beauty of every sort he adored. He was fond of display and loved the splendid. Certainly, he was arbitrary, for no one had ever disobeyed him. But he had a soft side, too—a part of him that hungered for affection. She had seen no fault in him today. He was still her hero; but she knew that whatever faults the future might reveal, she would love him just the same.

During the passing days while servants made the required changes in decor and Acratheus brought fabrics from which she was to choose draperies and upholsteries as well as her coronation robe and wedding garments, she still had idle moments when she would sit behind curtained windows gazing into the outer court.

Never before had she realized the terrific amount of duties imposed upon a monarch, for all these people came, hoping for an audience with the king. Sabuchadas told her that even when Ahasuerus retired, six scribes sat all night outside his door in readiness to be called into his chamber and transcribe messages at his dictation.

Among those who entered the public court she recognized Haman. He came each day, walking with a swagger. Before him everyone bowed low, some even knelt, as though this man were the king himself. She asked Malme to tell her about him.

Haman, Malme said, put enormous emphasis upon the fact that he was of royal blood, being the direct descendant of Agag, once king of the Amalekites.

"Haman," went on Malme, "lives with his wife and ten sons on the other side of the city in a mansion with a wide public court. His wife is a plain, elderly woman with a long, humped nose and knobby hands like claws. The sons are ugly, too, and they put on airs as though they were sons of the king. The family was poor and unknown when they came to Shushan about eight years ago. I know not what made the king, who is an astute man, single out Haman for special honor, but now everyone caters to that family, and Haman has grown rich since the king has chosen to elevate him. There is this to be said about Your Majesty's future lord—he does not give his affection often, but when he does he seems to be blind to that person's faults and will hear no evil of him."

"You say the prime minister is rich. You mean through graft?"

Malme glanced about to make sure no one was listening.

Then she spoke, her voice low. "Haman reaches greedy fingers into many matters. Through his recommendation an architect or an engineer can secure a fat contract or a butcher secure the king's patronage. And so it goes. No one dares to tell the king. Several have tried, but the king will hear nothing against his favorite, dubbing such tales evidence of jealousy."

"I must not interfere in this matter," said Esther, more to herself than her companion. "The king has known Haman longer than he has known me, and if I were to find fault with Haman this, too, might be interpreted as jealousy."

"In deciding not to interfere, you are wise. Someday, somehow, perchance His Majesty will find out what manner of man Haman is, and then I pity the king, for it is sad to know that one's trust has been misplaced."

When the time of the marriage feast arrived—a whole month of celebration—Esther took no part in it. The king held bachelor banquets each day. Esther could look out over the city and see the many lights, the torchlight processions, and she heard her name again and again. "Long live Queen Esther." She heard it hour after hour—in the high-pitched voices of children, in the hilarious voices of women and the sturdy voices of men.

Every day at her breakfast table she found a note from Ahasuerus.

"I am thinking of you, my bride, and my heart longs to embrace you," or, "Are you well, beloved? Sleep soundly this night and let your dreams tell you how deeply you are rooted in my affections."

She thought of Vashti. They said that these days Vashti, was sullen and aging rapidly. Had he ever sent such notes to her? Once, overcome with curiosity, she put the question to Malme.

"Vashti was evil," Malme replied. "She would have cared nothing for such messages. Now she's bitter and full of malice, and deep violet shadows are about her eyes—and nobody cares. Have no fear, Your Highness has blotted her image from his mind, just as you are now wiping out her taste from this house."

Never had Malme dressed her young mistress with more care than on the last day of the feast, the day of her wedding.

Long before noon the crowd began gathering in the outer court. Persian soldiers with their rectangular shields and short swords were stationed a few feet apart from each other to keep order. All races crowded the court.

Assyrian priests with their headdresses of bullock horns. Amalekites. Princes in flowing purple cloaks. Hebrews with prayer curls in front of their ears. Medians in silk with Scythian daggers. Dark-skinned Elamites. Egyptians with woolen wigs and artificial beards. Persian nobles in brocade. None of them knew, thought Esther as she gazed upon that restless throng, that the queen was an Israelite. They naturally assumed she was a Babylonian.

She was dressed much too early, and moved back and forth nervously from window to window. There was a wide cleared space about a platform which was covered by a white and blue canopy. She saw the servants light the braziers which held the sacred incense at the four corners of the structure. Then she saw the solemn priests coming in a procession from the king's own tabernacle in their white and purple aprons, with bare feet, shaved heads and tall ritual hats.

"It is time, Your Majesty," said Acratheus. "I beg you, do not look so sad. You are a bride! Smile! Hold your head high, your shoulders back. Malme, quick! A little more paint on her cheeks."

Esther felt stifled. She longed to tear the wide golden necklace from her throat. "All those people! Those staring eyes! Suppose I do something wrong?"

"A queen must grow used to people and staring eyes. The people want to love you. Look upon them with love and your fear will go."

She flung a wild, helpless look at him, and then walked slowly down the long flight of stairs. As she reached the door, Sabuchadas opened it for her. There was a blare of trumpets as, simultaneously, the door of the king's palace opened. Bride and groom walked up to the platform from different directions.

They met in the center. He was resplendently robed and wearing his crown, blazing with jewels. In his left hand he carried the scepter. The crowd was hushed now.

Later she did not remember the ceremony, except that it was mercifully short. From the rear came the music of stringed instruments, low and melodious. Chanting something to the music, a priest placed her hand in that of the king. Then the chief priest intoned some strange words. When he had finished, she thought with a wave of relief, "Thank God! Now it's over!"

But still the people did not move, nor did the king or the priests. She wondered why. The heat was oppressive. The smell of the incense was making her ill. The eyes of the priests were somber. A hot, dry wind arose, and now, above it, she heard the stirring of the crowd and a long, concerted "a—ah." She saw what had agitated them now. It was the crown being carried forward on a cushion. Hatach, who brought it, sank upon one knee lifting the pillow toward the king. Ahasuerus reached for the diadem and placed it on Esther's head. Then, taking her hand, he led her a few steps forward.

"Behold your queen!" he cried in a voice that rang out with pride and youth and joy.

The tension snapped. Pandemonium prevailed. The trumpets burst forth in a long, triumphant blare. The musicians broke into a lively tune. The people screamed with delight. They waved streamers of every hue. They shouted her name.

"Esther! Esther!"

"Star of Persia!"

"Incarnate goddess! Goddess of love and beauty!"

Ahasuerus smiled upon them. Then amid the cheers he led her across the court. Presently the heavy carved door of the queen's palace closed behind them.

8: A Stranger in Shushan

NO GIRL could want a more gallant, considerate husband. He admired all that she had done to the house, which had now taken on a freshness and a coolness the overfurnished rooms had lacked.

"I shall love coming here," he declared fervently, "for now the house speaks eloquently of you."

The honeymoon lasted only a week, and then the king returned to his own palace and the work which had been piling up awaiting his attention. Before leaving he coached Esther in her duties as queen. In Persia the queen was considered sacred, like a goddess. Only on her coronation and at such times as her husband requested it, could her face be seen by any other man. Tradesmen, who naturally desired the prestige of the queen's patronage, were not permitted to bring their wares directly to her. Instead, they were seen in the main hall by the head eunuch, who weeded out such things as he deemed worthy and then brought the various articles to the queen for her selection. She was not permitted to leave her palace for shopping or visiting, even behind the closed curtains of a litter, nor could she enter the king's palace without first receiving an invitation from him, but she must be ready to obey his summons and she must also be ready to receive him in her home whenever he found an opportunity to come.

Every window was curtained with a material which, though it let in the light and allowed her to see out, was opaque to those on the outside. These curtains by law could not be put aside. For instance, she could not peer out by parting the curtains by so much as an inch.

She would have at her disposal unlimited wealth. She could send to the king's library for any book she wished. She could receive any feminine friends she liked, but they must come only at her invitation and she must never return their calls.

At state banquets Ahasuerus always wanted her beside him. Only at these times did she meet the prime minister. Not wanting to displease her husband, she was gracious to this man.

Fermenting in Haman's mind at this time was a scheme which, if successful—so long as the king had no son—would put Haman on the throne. For months he toyed with the idea, not hinting of it even to his family.

Meanwhile, Esther's love for Ahasuerus and his devotion to her increased. She learned to be reconciled to the fact that sometimes a month passed and he neither summoned her nor visited her. But short notes passed frequently between them, and though she longed to see him more often, she wisely made no demands upon him.

One day, chancing to glance out of the window, she saw amid the crowd a familiar face. She gasped, telling herself that it couldn't be. She stared, then cried aloud, "It is! It's Uncle Mordecai!"

Her impulse was to push aside the curtains, lean out, invite him in. Then she recalled that this was forbidden.

He stood quietly, talking to no one, a distinguished-looking, middle-aged Hebrew in a scribe's turban. He looked older than she remembered him. All this time he had not been able to communicate with her, but with Acratheus as her ally she had written to him. Whenever a messenger left for Babylon on official business, Acratheus had made it his business to learn of it. Esther would write a letter and give it to the eunuch, who would give it to the messenger with a tip, explaining that this Mordecai who lived in the Hebrew section was a friend of his. And now Mordecai was in Shushan!

She rang a bell and Acratheus appeared. Excitedly, she drew him to the window and pointed downward.

"That tall man standing to the right of the gate, do you recognize him?"

"Yes, Your Majesty. It is that kind man, your uncle, whom I met in Babylon—Mordecai, the scribe."

"Yes, it is he. It is really he. Go to him at once. Tell him the rules of this place and how it is that I cannot invite him in or visit with him or offer him hospitality without my lord's permission. Ask him if he needs anything. Give him my love. Tell him I am well and wondrous happy. Find out what he is doing here. Then hasten back and tell me."

Standing by the window she saw Acratheus cross the court and approach Mordecai. They talked earnestly together, and with a discreet glance, Acratheus indicated the window where Esther was standing. Mordecai looked up at it and smiled. Sometime later, Acratheus, who was getting fatter every day, came puffing into the room, scarcely able to breathe from the exertion of climbing the stairs of the palace so hurriedly.

"What did he say? What did he say? How is he?"

"He is well. He says he loves you like his own daughter. He says that he has sold his house in Babylon and come thither intending to make Shushan his home in order to be near you. He says he is proud of you and rejoices in your happiness. He has found, he says, a pleasant room in a Jewish inn at the other side of town and is well cared for. He will establish his business here, coming each day to that spot near the gate so that you can send him word by me how you are. He says I am to make clear to the queen that he wants nothing from her, that he has all he needs. Your uncle forbids you to mention his presence to the king or make any attempt to receive him in your house."

"But why?"

"He said to remind you of the words he spoke to you when last he saw you."

"Oh. Oh, yes."

"The gentleman, your uncle, is a wise man. He knows how close an Amalekite is to the king. He says it is a wife's duty to keep strife from her house at all costs. The king, he said, has enough of that in his council chamber. Let him find, he says, only happiness, harmony, peace and love when he comes to you."

"Each day, then, at this time, you will take a message from me to him."

"I will. Have no fear. No one will suspect that he is related to Your Highness. They are accustomed to my coming and going, and often I stop to speak to friends who chance to be in the court."

She frowned. "I do not like being silent about my uncle. I am proud of Mordecai, and I am not ashamed of being a Hebrew. I would have told the king long ago, but before I left Babylon my uncle advised me not to."

"It is not a case of being ashamed, it is a question of wisdom. Under the circumstances your uncle is wise. Had you been my daughter I would have advised the same thing. Were you an ordinary woman it would be different. Fortunately, the king is tolerant in the matter of religion. He does not compel you nor does he even request you to attend his tabernacle or worship his god, Ahura-Mazda. He quite naturally assumes that coming from Babylon, you have your own gods. He is content that you shall worship them in your own way."

"True. He has never questioned me in this matter and I have never thought to mention it. We see each other so rarely, and when we do we have so many other things to talk about."

When Acratheus had gone, she returned to the window, but Mordecai had left. Now she seated herself to think this situation over. She thanked God there was freedom of worship in Persia. She was glad that Mordecai was near her, yet she was wretched that she could not invite him to share her home, as once he had taken her in and shared all that he had with her. And now that he was here in Shushan were they never to have any contact with each other? It was unthinkable. Why not talk honestly to her husband about this? They talked freely and honestly about everything else.

She hesitated only because of his closeness to Haman, and she saw that Haman, once he knew that she was a Jewess, could be an implacable foe. Remembering his dark, pointed face and beady eyes, he seemed to her more reptile than human, and she knew that he must be subtle as a serpent and clever as one, else he could not have retained his power over the king this long.

What to do? Tell Ahasuerus or not? Certainly, the thought of Mordecai, her only relative, standing outside her door day after day was distasteful. How much she owed him! Without his discipline and training she could never have found favor with the king, could never have worn the crown of Persia. Mordecai, in all justice, was entitled to the respect due him as the uncle of the queen.

So, though she respected his wisdom and valued the advice of Acratheus, her natural honesty kept prompting her to tell Ahasuerus the whole story when next she saw him. She knew that in all his empire no people were more loyal to him than the Hebrews. They had more cause to be grateful to him than any of the other races which he governed. Under his rule they had enjoyed freedom and prosperity.

Even as she thought of her husband, he came dashing up the stairs, his face flushed, his eyes glaring with fury. So incensed was he that she shrank from him in terror, unable to imagine that this man, who had always been so kind to her, so lovable and soft-spoken, could be capable of a temper so wild. For the first time she realized how tempestuous were his rages, and there arose in her a terrible fear of ever being the cause of such anger.

For a moment she sat, wide-eyed, frozen, while he strode up and down, exclaiming about a drought in Egypt, two of his ships being wrecked in a storm and, what was even more disastrous, a flood of the Indus.

What frightful news to come in a single day! She knew instinctively that he had not given vent to his wild rage before his subjects, but instead he had come to her. She did not know what to say to him, she did not know how to calm him. For a time she could do nothing but sit and watch him as he went tearing about.

"The flood!" he cried. "Needless! Thousands upon thousands I spent only last year to build a wall to prevent such mishaps, and at the first pressure the wall gives way. Hundreds perish! Oh, if I could get my hands upon that grafting engineer, I'd strangle him!"

"Did my lord interview this man before sending him to undertake this important work?"

"Of course I did. I questioned him and he was recommended to me highly."

"By whom?"

"By my best friend, Haman."

"Haman! Haman brought this man to you!"

Immediately, Esther saw how Haman had profited by the deal. Now, surely, Ahasuerus would see that his so-called friend was not to be trusted.

But no. Even as she thought this, Ahasuerus, as though reading her mind, spoke quickly, hotly, defensively.

"Ah, poor Haman! He was as deceived as I. He is desolated at the catastrophe. It was all I could do to prevent him from killing himself!"

Esther could imagine the scene which had taken place when the news had been reported. The tragic act put on by Haman! The feigned bitterness in his voice. The frenzy in his eyes. How could Ahasuerus fail to see that it had been all pretense? But wisely she said nothing. She only gazed with stricken, white face at the king as he sank upon a divan.

"Relief has been sent to the area?" she asked at last.

"Yes, yes. All night I've been working on this matter of sending relief, and all the while it seemed as if I could hear the cries and weeping of those poor people, who had blessed me and sent their poor gifts to me because I had built their wall. I have pledged not only to rebuild the wall but the whole area. Such a tragedy, such a waste. Crops gone. Homes swept away. Children killed. And besides this, comes news of some Hellenes stirring up a rebellion against me in Egypt. It is common knowledge that the Greeks would like to conquer Persia. Any border incident might provoke war. It takes all my diplomacy to avert it. The Greeks grow ambitious, envious as they are of Persia's wealth."

No, Esther decided, this was no time to tell him about Mordecai. So many other things of far greater importance made her own problems insignificant.

"I know," he went on, calm now, "that their spies are everywhere. And whom can I trust? How can I be certain that my own life is not in danger?"

"No! No! Do not say such things!"

"Why not? My own father was murdered in the palace by one whom he trusted. Rebellion! I know that Egypt is on the verge of rebellion, so is Syria and Media, rebellion against me. Beneath this peace there surges danger from all sides. Whom can I trust? Whom but you and Haman?" He looked across the room at her. "You will never bring me sorrow, beloved."

"Never. Never. Oh, let me not add so much as an ounce of weight to this fearful load you carry!" She went to him swiftly, sat beside him, touched his knee with her hand. "Oh, my lord, it has been so long since I have seen you! A whole week."

"I know. I know. An age."

"I have wanted to go to you."

He spoke forcefully. "You must never do that, Esther. Never. For though I died, I must uphold the law. You have never seen me on my days of audience. Listen. Let me explain how it is. About the throne stand ten guards with sharp, upraised axes. Should anyone— *anyone*— approach me whom I do not invite to do so, these guards would fall upon that person and immediately destroy him."

"There? Before your eyes?"

"Before my eyes. However, in public, I must always carry my scepter. If I choose, I hold this toward the person who has approached me, and he whom I touch with it is then out of danger. So you must never come to me. You must never attempt to put my love for you to the test. You must never expect me or ask me to break a law."

"I promise. I promise. Now then, lean back. Let me wipe that frown from your eyes. Indeed, I never dreamed my lord could be so fierce in anger. Seeing you like that petrified me with fear. If that anger should ever be directed against me— " She shivered.

"I have a bad temper, but I have learned to keep it under control most of the time. Forgive me if I have frightened you, but the load grows so heavy, my responsibilities are so great. That cursed, grafting engineer! What a costly mistake that was!"

"Do not think of it now. I am here to help you bear your troubles. Relax. Rest."

He closed his eyes and she began stroking his head with her cool, perfumed fingers, her heart overflowing with love and sympathy for this man who could be so fierce and yet so gentle.

"The storm in you has passed now," she said at last.

"Yes, it has passed. Here I can rest. Safety is here. There is strength in you. I do not mean physical strength, but another kind of strength." After a short pause, he rose. "I am calmer now. The ache in my head is gone."

"Must my lord leave me so soon?"

"I must. Hundreds of people, each with his individual problem, are waiting to see me. To them every minute of delay produces an eternity of suspense. From the mountains they come, and from the deserts, from the farms and from the cities. Besides, I have an appointment with a Greek sculptor who is to make a statue of me which I am expected to donate to Nineveh."

"But cannot my lord delay this meeting with the sculptor when so many other things—"

"I am a Persian, Esther," he said with pride. "We Persians are a peculiar people. We show no mercy to rebels or traitors, and we hate lying and liars. A Persian's word is sufficient. I have promised to give this sculptor time for his modeling, and no matter what happens, I cannot break my word."

"So be it, my lord."

She let him go, her mind filled with the thought of floods, droughts, rebellions moving stealthily and unseen; of Haman, that grafting politician. The thought came to her that troubles often come, not singly, but in a torrent.

And now she had a presentiment that there was even more trouble to come.

9: The Conspiracy

ESTHER awakened next morning still oppressed by a sense of foreboding. Even when, shortly after the noon meal, Malme brought her a new robe just finished by her sewing women, she viewed it lethargically, and in a toneless voice told Malme to put it in the closet. Then, motioning Malme to leave, she walked to the window and sat staring over the courtyard.

Haman was just arriving. Followed by servants and sycophants, he strutted through the crowd and the people made their obeisance before him.

Her face brightened when, a little later, she saw Mordecai take his place at the gate.

Acratheus had gone on an errand and she knew that he would stop on his return to tell Mordecai that she sent him her love. Mordecai looked in excellent health. Older, but still strong. For all his quietness and inconspicuous attire, there was an air of importance about him. She remembered how, as a little girl, she had always turned to Mordecai with her troubles. And now she saw someone else turn to him, someone obviously in trouble, too.

It was a short man who moved tensely and kept peering about as though afraid of being observed. He approached Mordecai and began to talk, though it was plain that they did not know one another. They talked earnestly, and Esther wondered what they were talking about. Mordecai looked grave. Esther saw him nod. Then with singular abruptness the short man left the court. Now Mordecai appeared worried. He kept moving his head from side to side as though impatient to see Acratheus.

Minutes lagged. There was a tenseness about Mordecai now. What was keeping Acratheus?

The afternoon passed and she fumed at the absence of her servant. Where was he? The sun was sinking and the crowd in the court was dwindling. Ah, there was Acratheus, hurrying as usual, and wiping the perspiration from his forehead. He stopped and spoke to Mordecai. Acratheus seemed to stiffen as Mordecai talked.

Then in a great rush he took leave of her uncle and hastened to the queen's palace. Mordecai left at once. A few minutes later, Acratheus was bowing before Esther.

"Where have you been all this time?" she asked.

"Your Majesty, I was delayed. I shall explain that later. Oh, this is terrible!"

"What is it? Something my uncle told you?"

"He told me of a plot to kill the king tonight! A man named Bar Nabazus had just told it to him. Your uncle said that you must find a way to warn His Majesty. You know the two men who have the title 'Keepers of the Door'?"

"Bigthan and Teresh. Yes."

"They have been in service upon the king for about eight years. They stand at the door when his meals are brought. They taste everything first. Now, the servant of Teresh, this Bar Nabazus, is a Hebrew."

"A short man?"

"Yes. Bar Nabazus overheard Bigthan and Teresh plotting how to do this thing! When Bar Nabazus was sure of not being detected, he made haste for the palace. He pleaded to see the king at once, but was told he would have to wait his turn."

"And so?"

"So he was desperate and knew not what to do." Acratheus, his eyes bulging more than ever, started mopping the perspiration from his throat. "And seeing your uncle standing at the gate and recognizing him as a fellow-Jew and thinking your uncle looked important and might have some entry to the king, Bar Nabazus told him the story about the plot to kill His Majesty tonight. Bar Nabazus learned of it only this morning. Since then he had tried to see the king without the knowledge of either Bigthan or Teresh. But the law is that no one sees the king unless he first tells the scribe at the door why he wants an audience. But Bar Nabazus could not tell the scribe why he wanted to see the king. He was afraid that the scribe might somehow be in the plot." Acratheus gave a gesture of despair with both plump, ringed hands. "He was frantic with worry, did not know what to do, and has no real proof against Bigthan and Teresh. Mordecai says you must at once make the king aware of the conspiracy."

"How? I cannot go to him unless he summons me. Now then, let me think. *You* will go! Yes. You will go to the scribe at the door. Explain that you are the servant of the queen. Say the queen has been taken suddenly ill. If you can convince him of this, he will probably submit your name to the king at once, and the king will see you without delay. Now then, when you see the king, ask that you speak to him in private, and when you are alone with him, tell him what Mordecai has said. Say to the king that it is my plea that he permit you to remain by his side until the truth of the matter is known. Only then will you return to me. You understand?"

Acratheus nodded.

"Go then. Go quickly!"

A few minutes later she saw him enter the king's palace. The guard recognized him as the queen's personal servant and ordered those who loitered in the anteroom to make way for him. Acratheus had now a clear passage to the scribe who sat at the door of the throne room. At sight of him the man knew at once that something was wrong. Acratheus was pale and he moved with urgency. Obviously he was filled with fright.

"Tell the king I have a message from the queen. It cannot wait. Her Majesty is taken suddenly ill. This is a matter of life or death!"

The man hesitated, looked at the door to the throne room, then back at Acratheus again.

"Do not delay," fumed Acratheus. "If you do, a life will pay for it and lie like a blot upon your soul!"

The scribe beckoned a soldier and relayed the message, telling him to knock upon the door. From the inside, the door was opened by a servant, to whom the soldier repeated the words which the scribe had said to him.

"Your Majesty," said the servant, "it is the queen's eunuch. He has an urgent message from the queen and implores the king to see him at once, saying that the queen is taken suddenly ill, and it is a matter of life or death."

About the throne stood the axemen, weapons poised. Near the king was Haman.

"Let him in at once!" shouted Ahasuerus excitedly.

Hearing the words, Acratheus entered the throne room. Trained from babyhood for service in the palace, he had been taught to move quickly, for royalty must never be kept waiting. His bulk was no deterrent to this speedy motion as he covered the long expanse from the door to the throne.

Before he could kneel, the king spoke. "The queen! What is it?"

"Your Majesty, this—it is something for your ears alone. I implore you, a moment of your time in the name of the queen!"

It was impossible to doubt the earnestness of the speaker. Puzzled and alarmed the king motioned Acratheus to accompany him into a closetlike room behind the throne. When Acratheus had carefully closed the door, the king addressed him worriedly.

"Now, what is it? Speak quickly. What has befallen the queen?"

"Not the queen, Your Highness. It is danger to yourself. It is already late. A delay would be fatal. The queen told me to say she was ill. It was a device to get through to Your Majesty, for the matter will not wait."

Ahasuerus was calm now, a cold calmness that seemed to drop over him like a shield, giving the impression that he was detached from whatever Acratheus might say. With as few words as possible, Acratheus told the king of the plot.

"Mordecai?" the king frowned. "Mordecai? I have never heard of him. It is a Babylonish name. Who is this man?"

"Your Majesty, he is a stranger in Shushan. Scarcely a week ago he arrived here from Babylon. He is a friend of mine whom I met in Babylon during my stay there on Your Majesty's business. Since then from time to time I have been in touch with him, and I can vouch for his loyalty. However, it is well to point out that whether this thing be true of false, Mordecai cannot know, but it seemed to him that quick action was compulsory in order to prove the story either fact or falsity. It may be that the servant of Teresh has some grudge against his master and is lying. My friend Mordecai pointed out to me that he does not know the fellow, but he insisted that I tell the queen the story and prayed that the queen might reveal the tale to the king at once."

"A wise and estimable man, this Mordecai."

"Now then," went on Acratheus, as though the king had not spoken, "when I repeated to the queen what Mordecai had said, she commanded that I warn my lord the king, and begs the king that he will permit me to remain with him until—until the truth be proven."

"I commend the queen and you. I am deeply indebted to this stranger, Mordecai. Bigthan and Teresh! Why, they were born on these grounds! It is difficult to believe that they are conspirators. Yet how can I find out? What can I do to trap them? What shall I do to prove either their guilt or innocence?"

"Since they serve Your Majesty's meals, could their weapon be poison?"

Ahasuerus leaned against one of the colonnades, and his handsome face, though thoughtful, was devoid of agitation.

"Probably poison," he admitted at last. "Either that or a dagger while I sleep. But I cannot believe this of them."

"Your Majesty, in pity for the queen do not send me from you. Her Highness begs you to permit me to remain by you. She will be frantic unless there is someone near you in this hour whom she can trust."

"So be it. Remain until this is settled. We will return to the throne room. Stand near me so that you may hear all that is said and report to my lady what transpires."

Ahasuerus faced the door and Acratheus sprang forward to open it. The king returned to the dais, his face inscrutable, his manner serene.

Haman's eyes were upon him fixedly, as if trying to read his thought. "The queen is not seriously ill?" he asked.

The royal eyes rested appreciatively upon Haman. "My faithful Haman! The one man whom I can really trust! No, thank heaven, the queen is well." Never had Acratheus admired his king more heartily than at this time when, faced with the possibility of being murdered before nightfall, he was utterly fearless. He addressed the guards. "Men, be at ease. Go to the far end of the room and remain there until I call you. Say to the scribe outside that I will see no one else today. Anyone who waits in the anteroom is to be dismissed."

When his bodyguard was beyond hearing distance, Ahasuerus spoke to Haman in a low voice. "I have learned a thing that is somewhat surprising."

Haman lifted his thin eyebrows and waited, guardedly, suspiciously, for the king to speak again.

"I have learned of a plot to kill me," announced Ahasuerus with less emotion than he would have shown had he been told that the sun would rise in the morning.

Haman started. "When?"

"Tonight," replied Ahasuerus casually.

Watching Haman, Acratheus saw his face grow white, a sickly, grayish white. All dignity had departed. Can he, thought Acratheus, really love the king that much?

"No!" cried Haman. "No, Your Majesty, this cannot be! This is impossible. Someone is trying to frighten the king. Do not put credence in such wild, unlikely tales. How—who—?"

Now, with a swordlike thrust, another thought forced its way into the mind of Acratheus. Could it be—could it be that Haman was in the conspiracy? Could this agitation be for himself and not the king?

And why not? With the king dead, and having no son in line for the throne, how easily could Haman, the prime minister, take over the army and come into power! Was his trembling due to the fact that he feared that his guilt was about to be discovered? Ahasuerus, too, was not blind to Haman's trembling, and sought to pacify him.

"Now, now, father, your concern proves your love for me. As if I needed proof on that score! But have no fear. We may find a way to trap the conspirators."

Haman relaxed a trifle. "Conspirators! Who—who are these men?"

"Bigthan and Teresh."

Haman smiled. "Oh, not they, my lord! Surely Your Majesty would not suspect them? Where could such a ridiculous tale have come from? Now then, Your Majesty, do not trouble yourself about it further." Haman's voice was caressing. "I pray you, sire, let the matter rest in my hands. I will investigate. I will find out the truth. Let me handle this for Your Majesty. Your Majesty knows that his life is more precious to me than my own, that the moments spent in his presence are my only real delight."

Acratheus felt his blood surge into his face. He said nothing, but inwardly he spoke to his king. "Do not be ensnared by this! Do not let yourself be deceived!"

Ahasuerus was smiling. "Good old Haman! But it is better that we see this through together."

"I—I beg Your Majesty's leave to go and —"

"No. Stay with me, friend."

Ahasuerus was silent for a long time. Haman grew more and more nervous as the silence continued. He glanced toward the door as if longing to escape. Several times his thin face was distorted by an involuntary twitching. The silence was intolerable to him. He could bear it no longer.

"What—er—what is Your Majesty p-planning to do?" he asked at last.

"I am thinking how to trap them. What does my good friend advise?"

"I—I'm so devastated at the thought of anything happening to Your Majesty, that I—I cannot think clearly. I know not what to advise. It is of no use to summon and question them, since if they are guilty they would only lie."

"No, questioning will avail us nothing. We must have proof. We cannot convict on hearsay. We have only the word of Teresh's servant."

"If Your Highness sent for that servant of Teresh's—but—remember, my lord, that the man might have some grudge against Teresh! In fact, it may well be a plot to get Teresh into trouble."

"True, and I must be fair."

"How did this report come to your ears?" asked Haman of Acratheus.

"Sir, as I was today on an errand for Her Majesty, a man, a friend of mine, stopped me. He is a stranger in the city and was loitering at the gate hoping for a glimpse of the king, as do all strangers when first they come to Shushan. He told me the story, insisting that by some means I must reach the king before it was too late, since the plot is in some way to be carried out tonight."

A sneer spread over Haman's thin face. "Oh? And how had this stranger heard the tale?"

"He had it from Teresh's servant, Bar Nabazus."

"Bar Nabazus! Ah! A Hebrew name! And why should Bar Nabazus tell it to this complete stranger?"

"Because," replied Acratheus, choosing his words carefully, "he was desperate and had to tell someone."

Haman spoke mockingly. "There's a Hebrew for you! Pushing. Unscrupulous. They always stir up trouble. Your Majesty has no doubt heard of the saying of my people, 'Never trust a Jew.' That is because to our misfortune we have had dealings with them in the past. They are shrewd, tricky, treacherous, lying, underhanded—"

"This is no time to discuss the character of the Hebrews," the king answered quietly. "I can see now how I have played into the hands of Bigthan and Teresh. No doubt they have waited a long time for just such a night as this."

"How so, Your Majesty?" asked Haman.

"As you know, I scarcely ever dine alone. Sometimes you and I dine with few or many, but this morning when I summoned Teresh to order the day, I told him that tonight I would be served with a light repast in my chamber and would retire at once. So, if he is a conspirator, this is just such an opportunity as he has been desiring."

"But—"

"Are you suddenly blind, Haman? You see what would happen. Bigthan and Teresh would serve the meal. I would be alone with them. I would either be drugged so that I would be defenseless and they would plunge a knife into my heart, or I would drop dead with poison. They would then put me in my bed so that I would appear to be sleeping. Outside, the six scribes who always sit at my door, would remain throughout the night. In the morning, when it seemed that I was slumbering later than my custom, no one would dare disturb me. It would grow later. Finally someone would be sufficiently brave to knock upon the door. Receiving no answer, he would not presume to enter because of the law which says that no one can approach royalty unless royalty bids them do so. So the man would go away. But inevitably as the day wore on, someone would think I was ill, and if they cared sufficiently, they would break the law and enter the room, only to find me dead. By that time the conspirators could have gotten so far away that it would be impossible to apprehend them."

Ahasuerus had addressed Haman, leaving Acratheus free to let his gaze wander from one face to the other.

The face of the young monarch was as calm as though he were discussing some minor change in his gardens. The aging face of the prime minister was taut. His hands clenched and unclenched. His eyes were glittering. Yet when he spoke, his voice was flattering and humble.

"The king of Persia has the wisdom of the gods, the insight of the immortals. May he live forever. May the gods watch over him and preserve him. May his power increase. May all traitors perish. May his kingdom extend to the ends of the earth. If it please the king, most noble young lion, let me have these men arrested instantly. Let me put them to trial. Let me call Bar Nabazus and this—this stranger, whatever his name is, as witnesses, and by heaven, if they have lied—"

Yes, thought Acratheus, and if you are implicated in the plot, you will intimidate and torture Mordecai and Bar Nabazus and end by exonerating the two stewards. He waited tensely for the king's reply.

"That will not be necessary," said Ahasuerus. "I myself will bring them to trial, and tonight!"

Haman was meek and ingratiating. "Is it my king's wish to tell his humble and devoted vassal how?"

"You, my friend, will be a witness to the proceeding, you and this faithful minion of the queen." The fine, royal face was determined, but it was still devoid of agitation. "Guards!"

The ten men who had been standing at the end of the room came forward in formation, their stout axes held in front of them with both hands, one hand above the other. Ahasuerus addressed each in turn, beginning with the man on the extreme left. His commands were crisp and calm.

"Yesterday among the gifts sent by foreign potentates was a small monkey. It pleases me to have this animal amuse me for a few hours. Go forthwith to the keeper of my creatures and say that I wish it to be brought to my bedchamber at once."

The soldier bowed and, still bowing, backed out of the room. "And you," commanded that voice of calm authority, "remove my crown and deliver it to the keeper of my treasures." Ahasuerus did not, however, relinquish his scepter, which he must always either carry or keep close at hand, even while he slept. "And you, go to the keeper of my bedchamber. Say that the king is worn with the travail of this day and would retire early. He is therefore to prepare my bath, my bed and my night robes at once." He addressed the man next in line. "And you, go to my trusted stewards, Bigthan and Teresh. Say that the king is wearied and dines lightly, alone in his room. They are to serve my supper there after my bath." Speaking now to the fifth man, he said, "And you, seek out the six scribes who are to be on duty tonight. Tell them to take their places outside my door."

Five soldiers remained, expecting to be dismissed for the night. The king spoke to them collectively, his words including Haman and Acratheus. "Come with me."

Ahasuerus led the way out of the throne room. By tacit acknowledgement of Haman's right to be closest to the king, Acratheus and the guards stood aside, permitting the prime minister to precede them. They traversed a long stone corridor where at intervals burly attendants stood with lighted torches which so thoroughly illumined the way that the mosaic work on the floor was displayed in all its rich colorings, and the intricate carvings on doorways and staircases stood out in bold relief. On the way they passed no one but these figures who stood like statues against the stone wall. The king, the prime minister, Acratheus and the guards mounted the stairway, finally stopping before a door which Acratheus sprang forward to open.

The room was lighted only by the courtyard flares. In one corner was a large bed of carved silver with canopy and draperies of blue and lavender silk. Here and there were tall, richly carved vases filled with fresh flowers. Their fragrance blended pleasantly with the odors of myrrh, aloes and cinnamon with which the royal bed was always perfumed. A large and ornate chair with a tall back was near one of the windows. Close to it was a table of ebony and ivory. Its top was upheld by ebony feminine figures from which flowed a graceful pattern of scarves carved in ivory. Ahasuerus addressed the soldiers. "You are to conceal yourselves in that closet until I call you. Remember, not a whisper, not a sound."

If the men were puzzled by this order, their faces remained expressionless as they obeyed. When they had gone, Ahasuerus turned to Haman and Acratheus. "Conceal yourselves behind the draperies of the bed."

Haman opened his mouth to speak, but evidently thought better of it. When he and Acratheus were hidden, the king sat in the high-backed chair, sighed, and resting one elbow on the arm of it, cupped his chin in his hand. The big room was silent as a tomb, but unlike a tomb, the silence was pervaded by uneasiness. The hush seemed to spread out, beyond the room into the night, for not a bird sang, not a leaf rustled.

Acratheus was relieved when the stillness was broken at last by a knock on the door. Receiving the king's permission to enter the servant of the bedchamber came in, followed by several other men carrying a large water-filled tub, lamps and towels. The tub was placed upon the floor and while four men helped to disrobe the king, another turned back the coverlet of the bed. Acratheus and Haman held their breaths, involuntarily moving closer together.

They breathed easier when the task was finished and the servant walked away from the bed. Acratheus was aware that Haman was having difficulty in keeping still. At the prime minister's girdle was a short Persian sword. Nervously, he kept fingering its hilt.

The servants were slow, quiet and deliberate in all that they did. Ahasuerus submitted to their ministrations with no indication of impatience. As he lay stretched out in the golden tub, they anointed his beard and brushed his black, curly hair. Then his long, lithe body was scrubbed with some fragrant soap. Even Acratheus was impatient now, finding this wait intolerable. Beside him, Haman was trembling, and Acratheus said to himself, "This man, this bully, this braggadocian Amalekite, is a coward. Is he afraid because he fears for the king's life or because of something presently to be revealed about himself?" There was no way of knowing.

As the king's body was being dried with sweetly scented towels, a slight noise was heard outside the door as the scribes placed their portable tables in the hall and squatted near them on the floor.

When the royal bath was finished and Ahasuerus was in his night clothes, the tub, the brushes, the towels and the ointments were taken away. The king returned to the large chair, picked up a report that lay on the table and was apparently studying it when there came another knock on the door. This time it was the keeper of the creatures, who was leading a bright-eyed brown monkey on a chain. The monkey, gibbering excitedly as though he knew this was some extraordinary occasion, perched audaciously upon the arm of the king's chair. Ahasuerus smiled and patted him.

"Leave him here. He amuses me."

Ahasuerus himself fastened the monkey's chain to his chair and the keeper of the creatures backed out of the room. Again Ahasuerus picked up the paper and sat reading it. Almost immediately there was another knock. It was Bigthan and Teresh, both carrying trays which they put upon the table, being elaborately concerned that each dish was placed just so.

The king was jovial. "Greetings, Bigthan. Greetings, Teresh." "O King," they said in chorus, "live forever."

"I have just been studying this report. No famine this year, plenty of wheat and sugar to store and to export. A fine fruit harvest, too. A goodly yield of barley. A rich shipment of wool to Greece. Hides and silk in abundance." Obviously, he was talking to keep the two in suspense.

"Er—ah—Your Majesty's dinner is getting cold," said Bigthan in a soft, honeyed voice.

"Umm,' went on Ahasuerus as though he had not heard, "a profitable load of carpets on the quays ready for shipment. Shawls, embroideries—er—what was it you said, Bigthan?"

"I ventured to remark that Your Majesty's food was cooling and is getting unpalatable."

Ahasuerus put aside the paper and smilingly indicated the monkey. "You see, I have a companion in my loneliness tonight. Ugly, but interesting, eh?"

The two men smiled. "Most interesting, Your Majesty." Still in no apparent hurry, the king looked down at the food.

"Ah! Just what I wished for! I shall sleep well tonight."

"May Your Majesty's rest be undisturbed," said Teresh. Bigthan stood with parted lips, his eyes upon the king, who now picked up a piece of barley bread and began idly breaking it into morsels.

The monkey, also interested in the food, jumped on the king's shoulder and peered at the dishes greedily. The two servants stood by, alert, ready to serve, while the king dipped a morsel of the bread slowly, slowly, into the dish of roast kid which had been cut in small pieces and was immersed in a sauce.

He spoke smilingly to the monkey. "And are you hungry, too, little friend?" He held a tidbit toward the animal.

"Your Majesty!" cried Teresh. "Forgive my boldness, but I have heard it said that such food does not agree with monkeys."

"So?" the king's smile widened. He seemed to be weighing carefully what his steward had said. "Nonsense, Teresh," he scoffed at last. "If I can eat it, then surely my young friend can eat it." He gave the succulent tidbit to the monkey. "There, little man. See, he likes it!"

Acratheus heard Haman give a choked sound as though he were having difficulty with his breathing. The eyes of Teresh and Bigthan were fixed in veiled anguish upon the animal, which hopped upon the tall back of the king's chair, then to the arm of it, as though eager for more. Again Ahasuerus reached for a morsel, and the monkey hopped delightedly upon the edge of the table. Then, so suddenly that Haman uttered a little cry, the animal gave a strangely human moan, fell to the floor and lay still.

Ahasuerus rose. The two stewards sank groveling at his feet, their faces white, their voices shrill. They writhed in fear.

"Your Majesty, I swear—"

"Your Majesty—"

"Guards!" called the royal voice. "Scribes!"

The five soldiers rushed from the closet and pounced upon the quivering, sobbing stewards.

The scribes brought in their tables and, squatting before them, began writing hurriedly. Haman and Acratheus emerged from their hiding place and stood at one side of the room.

"Pity!" moaned the stewards. "Pity!"

"Which of you placed the poison in that food?" demanded Ahasuerus. There was a pause. "Speak! Or I shall have you hacked to death on the spot!" .

"I swear by the gods I am innocent," screamed Bigthan, and pointed wildly at Teresh. "It was he!"

"Miserable liar!" shouted Teresh. "It was you! I swear I knew nothing of it! I swear, Your Majesty, by my soul I swear I knew nothing of this thing! It was Bigthan!"

"You are lying!" shrieked Bigthan hysterically.

"Enough of this," said Ahasuerus. "We have proof. We have their confessions. The scribes have taken down all that was said." He looked at Bigthan, who was now in such a state of terror that his eyes were glazed and his mouth dripped saliva. "Whose idea was it to murder me? Who else is implicated in this?"

In agony, Bigthan pointed a shaking finger at Haman. "His! His! He planned it! He! He promised us gold and protection!"

Haman leaned toward him, his dark face purple with rage. "You liar. You craven. You dog. You fiend out of Hades! You dare accuse me?

"Your Majesty knows that I value his life above my own. Your Majesty cannot believe for one moment that I—I, who owe Your Highness so much, would do this! Why, if I thought my lord the king suspected me of such treachery, I swear I would plunge this dagger into my heart before your very eyes!"

Ahasuerus shook his head. "Would I be such a fool as to take the word of liars and murderers against the word of my trusted old friend? I beg of you, Haman, do not concern yourself."

"It was he," shouted Teresh. "I swear! I swear!"

"Silence!" cried Ahasuerus. "Not content with your own ruin must you drag the prime minister down with you?"

Haman gave a deep, martyrlike sigh. "Because I am honored with Your Majesty's friendship I am hated and envied throughout the empire. These are the things I have to endure.

This is the price I pay for my love for the king. Now Your Majesty sees for himself the treachery I have to contend with!"

"Take these men away," ordered Ahasuerus to the soldiers. "And before I enter the throne room tomorrow I shall visit the place of execution and I shall expect to see their bodies hanging from the gallows."

Bigthan and Teresh, screaming, struggling, sobbing, pleading incoherently, were each in the strong hands of two soldiers. Ahasuerus addressed the fifth soldier, pointing to the dead monkey.

"Take the carcass out and bury it."

The man picked up the animal and left.

"Your Majesty," began Haman, all dignity and sorrow now, "this night I have been accused of treachery. I will, therefore, at once resign my position and exile myself from the beauty and joy of the king's noble presence forever."

"Nonsense, Haman, nonsense. Do you think I would take the word of those wretches before yours?" He walked over and put his hand affectionately upon Haman's bony shoulder.

Haman's thin lips were dry, and he moistened them with a quick movement of his tongue. "Your Majesty exonerates me completely?" And Acratheus knew that he was mindful now of the scribes who were making official records of the incident.

"Completely."

"To be banished from the grace and kindness of Your Majesty's radiant presence would kill me!" Haman was feeling sure of himself again. "It unnerves me to think of Your Majesty's life being in one moment's danger. I commend Your noble Majesty for his prudence. I am astounded that a thing like this could happen. I am old, and the old cannot stand grief as the young can."

Ahasuerus spoke heartily. "Go home and rest, Haman. It is over. Think no more of it."

"May the gods preserve and guard the king forever." .

Vital, young, confident of his friend, Ahasuerus smiled. "I thank you, father. And now you have my leave to return to your home. May your rest be as easy and as safe as mine will be."

"I am honored by the king's trust. I will offer sacrifices to my god in gratitude for his deliverance."

How, asked Acratheus, could the king look into that shrewd face and not perceive its cunning? But Ahasuerus was loyal and patient with those he loved and could see no wrong in them. Someday, thought Acratheus, someday he will find Haman out, and that day will be a bitter one for him.

"Go now, Haman. Sleep well."

Haman backed toward the door.

The king turned to Acratheus when the prime minister had gone. "In the box near the bed are my jewels. Tomorrow come and choose what you like from it as a reward for your service this night. And let this payment go into the records. Now then, take away that food and see that it is destroyed. Report to the queen what has taken place. Say that I commend her for her timely warning. Assure her that all danger is passed."

"Thank heaven!" breathed Acratheus feelingly, as he picked up the trays.

"And tomorrow, after getting a note from one of these scribes, go to my treasurer. Say to him that he is to pay one hundred pounds of gold to Bar Nabazus and have him trained as a Keeper of the Door in the place of Teresh."

"So be it, Your Highness."

When Acratheus had gone, the king sat in the chair and looked down at the scribes who, having recorded the scene, the date and every word that had been spoken, gazed up at him awaiting more dictation.

"The man who has really saved my life this night," said Ahasuerus at last, "is named Mordecai. Write down the name. Now I am thinking what reward I shall give this Mordecai, for it is impossible that one should do so fine a service to his king and not be richly rewarded. But what reward is great enough? He has saved my life!" Ahasuerus tilted his head back against the chair and closed his eyes. But before he spoke again his thought was interrupted by the sound of feet rushing along the corridor. He opened his eyes and felt a chill of apprehension. "What now?" he murmured. "What more?"

A hurried knock on the door, and he called a command to enter. It was a cavalry officer.

"Your Majesty, forgive the intrusion, but I thought this news should not be delayed."

"Well? Well?" Ahasuerus fixed upon him lively and inquiring eyes.

"Another border incident. This time near the Danube."

"Against my orders! What madness possesses these men! The fools! What are the casualties?"

"A hundred killed on our side. Fifty wounded. About two hundred dead of the foreigners."

The scribes wrote at furious speed as Ahasuerus began snapping out orders.

It was late when the officer left. Only then did the king recall Mordecai.

"I shall attend to this Babylonian some other time. For the present, enter his name in the records and bid him stay around the palace. As soon as I can, I shall reward him properly."

But next day, after viewing the bodies of Bigthan and Teresh hanging on the gallows, Ahasuerus turned his attention to the border incident.

And Mordecai was forgotten.

10: The Serpent Strikes

IT HAD been Mordecai's way to come to the main gate briefly, waiting only long enough to receive the eunuch's report about Esther and go away again. So far he had not seen the famous Haman. But now the king had bade him stay around the palace; consequently, he must remain in the court each day from morning till sundown.

"Say to Mordecai," said Esther to Acratheus, "that the king will surely reward him handsomely."

Mordecai sent back word that he was the king's servant and wanted no reward. What he had done had been only his duty, and a man should not be rewarded for that.

"Tell your queen that I forbid her to mention this matter to His Majesty. Tell her that I say she is to keep out of this affair. I am content as I am. I need nothing more than I have. I thank God the king was spared. Tell her to do likewise, and be happy and make him happy and keep well. That is all I ask."

Esther decided to obey. Knowing the king's generosity, she was sure that at some future time he would deal well with Mordecai. She knew, too, that if her husband and her uncle ever came to know one another they would be friends. She waited patiently for this, going about her tasks with a sense of gratitude and well-being.

But while Esther laughed and sang, sinister things were taking place in the public court.

Before Haman's entrance, he was always preceded by men with long whips crying out, "Clear the way for the prime minister! Make way for the prime minister of Persia whom the king delights to honor!" Immediately all the people fell back respectfully, then they either knelt or bowed low while Haman passed, followed by several servants.

The first time Mordecai heard the words, "Make way for the prime minister!" he was amazed at the singular vibration which rippled like magic over the entire court. People stiffened. Voices hushed. Laughter ceased. The crowds fell back, even trampling without apology on one another's toes, to form a wide center aisle. It was as if this man were held in awe.

The person next to Mordecai whispered, "It is the prime minister! Bow down, stranger, bow low, and remain so until he has passed!"

At first Mordecai was only aghast at the changed atmosphere in the court, and he looked about him in utter amazement, for the people were actually groveling!

"Kneel!" whispered the man. "It is His Majesty's will that everyone should bow before the prime minister. Why do you transgress the king's commandment?"

If it were the king's commandment, then it was a law—and Mordecai had always had the utmost respect for the laws of the land. He sometimes prostrated himself before his God. He would have knelt before the king—and, since he loathed being conspicuous, he would have knelt before the prime minister, but Haman was an Amalekite; every Amalekite was his enemy—and to kneel before an enemy!

He fought with himself. He reminded himself that it was the law and he must do it.

And yet he could not.

Old antagonism—old, older than himself, antagonism hundreds of years old—surged up in him and held him in an iron grip. It was stronger than his own common sense. It was stronger than his own will. Even knowing that the king had ordered it, Mordecai *could* not do this thing.

Haman was passing now. Mordecai alone remained upright.

The sharp eyes of the Amalekite glared. They took in the scribe's turban, the Hebraic ritual tassels on the coat, the prayer curls. The prime minister hesitated, apparently about to order Mordecai to kneel. Then, as though it were beneath his dignity even to address this Hebrew, he proceeded into the inner court. There he turned to one of his servants, his voice frigid and his eyes snapping with hatred.

"You saw that Hebrew who did not bow?" The servant nodded.

"Find out about him."

Sometime later the servant returned. "My lord, I could find out little about that man except that he is a stranger. He is a scribe named Mordecai, lives in the Hebrew quarter, has no family, and seems not to know anyone in Shushan."

"Does he not know that it is the custom to bow before His Majesty's prime minister?"

"He knows, sir."

"He knows—and refuses to obey! Huh! What *are* these Hebrews? Only a few years ago they were brought to Babylon as slaves. Now, by the gods, this is infuriating! A Hebrew! What are they but captives still? And the king treats them like free men! Oh, I hate them! I hate the whole filthy race!"

He paced back and forth indignantly. This was an unbearable situation. The *Persians* bowed before him. They worshipped him almost as if he were king.

But this detestable Hebrew refused him homage! He could not permit a thing like this to continue. Why, if the people saw that this Hebrew did not bow and yet went unscathed, in time everyone would refuse to bow! Something had to be done. This Mordecai had to be punished, and publicly, as an example.

Haman's servant, being a kindly man, went out into the court and spoke to Mordecai. "Stranger, if you would not cause trouble for yourself, I pray you bow when next the prime minister passes!"

"I cannot," answered Mordecai feelingly. "I simply cannot make myself do it!"

"Then take my advice and be absent from the court when he arrives and leaves."

"Yes, that would be wise, but I cannot do that, either. I wish to heaven I could, but the king has commanded me to remain."

"But why do you *not* bow? If others can do it, why not you?"

"I do not know," replied Mordecai unhappily. "There is no reason—except that I am a Hebrew and he is an Amalekite."

"Yes, I have heard of that old feud. Still, others of your race kneel before this man. It must be hard for them, but they do it."

"I know," Mordecai admitted miserably. "But somehow, I—I simply cannot."

"Well, unless you can bring yourself to bow, you will no longer be safe in Shushan. I warn you, the prime minister is a hard and vengeful man, and Hebrews are his particular detestation! You are simply asking for trouble. Be wise. Either get out of Shushan at once or—"

"I thank you for the warning, friend, but come what may, I cannot bring myself to bow before an Amalekite!"

"I have always heard it said that you Hebrews are a stubborn, stiff-necked people," muttered the man as he walked away.

All day Haman brooded upon the matter. The more he thought of it, the more his fury increased. When he left the palace that afternoon Mordecai was still there, standing tall and straight. Haman passed swiftly, apparently without seeing him.

What, Haman kept asking himself, shall I do about this? No Hebrew can triumph over *me*! It must not go on. He reasoned that it was too small a thing to ask the king to punish one man merely because that man did not bow. He talked the problem over with his wife and sons, who saw only one solution—secretly engage someone to kill the upstart Hebrew as he walked in some lonely street after nightfall.

Haman considered this, knowing with what ease it could be accomplished, but in the end he rejected it. If that were done, no one would realize that Mordecai had been punished because he failed to show proper respect to the prime minister. They would think he had been set upon by robbers or had engaged in a street fight. No, he must think of some other way to punish him.

For hours Haman pondered the question. Next morning Mordecai was in his accustomed place, but still he did not bow.

"Does he think he is as good as I am?" fumed Haman. "I have power. Shall it be said that I have no power over one Hebrew?"

Power over one Hebrew? Power over all of them! Power! Then why not use it? Exultantly, Haman repeated the words. Why not use my power? And why use it to punish *one* Hebrew? Use it to wipe out the whole lot of them! Use it to repay the humiliation they have caused my people in the past!

Haman's nerves quivered with excitement at the thought.

It brought him a kind of intoxication, so that his hands grew unsteady. When his wife spoke to him he was gruff and preoccupied. He was eager now to begin the slaughter. He schemed how he would talk to the king about it. The idea held him fascinated. Yes, purge the empire of the Hebrews. Once the Amalekites had been humbled and destroyed by them, but the wheel had turned. Now an Amalekite could pay them back. Haman would be miserable now until this was accomplished.

Kill them. Kill them all. And the sound of their screams would be sweet music in his ears. The more he thought of it, the more intoxicated he became with the realization of his own power. All morning he sat in council, saying little, only waiting for the time when he could talk to Ahasuerus alone.

The day passed and that opportunity did not come. When he left the palace that evening Mordecai still stood, the one in all the crowd who did not even lower his head. Haman scarcely slept that night. Next day he passed Mordecai again, and now he was on fire with impatience to have this matter concluded. He was overjoyed when Ahasuerus invited him to lunch and said that they would be alone. And now, here was his chance.

"It is good," said Ahasuerus, when they were seated at table, "to be alone with my friend. But you look worried, father. This is a day for gladness." He glanced out of the window. "See how the sun shines upon the almond trees. What? Not even a nod of agreement? Is something troubling you?"

Here was the opportunity Haman wanted. "Your Majesty is discerning. Yes, I am worried. The truth is, for a long time I have been troubled about a certain matter. I know full well that my king has enough worry as it is, and from my heart I am loth to add to it, but now I *must* speak, for this is of deepest concern to my beloved Persia! I would be disloyal if I failed to bring it to Your Majesty's attention."

"Speak freely. What is it?"

"Greatest of all kings, in our midst there is a certain nation, greedy and wicked. This nation is dispersed throughout your entire dominion. It is a nation which keeps itself separate from all others. Their laws are different from those of other people. They do not obey the king's laws, therefore what does it profit Your Majesty to permit such rebels to exist in your realm?"

"Those who refuse obedience to the laws of the country in which they live are liabilities to that country."

"Potential danger—exactly! This proud and unsociable group, in their manners, in their practices, in their unscrupulous way of doing business, has made enemies of your people. Everybody hates them. Now, your prime minister, though by birth an Amalekite, is a loyal Persian. He is a man whom his king has honored by calling 'friend' and 'father.' Is it not true that Your Majesty has ordered that all men should honor him whom you honor?"

"It is true. He whom the king honors must be honored by the people. The position of the prime minister is high. It is next to my own in the land. Authority is nothing unless the. people respect it."

"So. And the foreigners and the Persians do honor me. They are loyal and obedient to Your Majesty. But this nation of which I speak is disloyal and disobedient!"

"I will tolerate no disobedience to law!"

"Precisely. As I was saying, these people do not respect me, therefore they do not respect *you*! Why, even today I passed one of them in the outer court and he did not so much as bow his head! That is the type of people they are. They have their own laws and they openly, insolently, defy yours!"

The face of the young king was pained. "A people living under my protection and defying my laws! I knew not that such things were going on."

"Who is to tell the king but the king's friend, who speaks honestly and in the interests of Persia? Your Majesty is a benefactor to his subjects. Then he will give order to destroy these people utterly—utterly! Wipe them all out! Your Majesty knows that the country is in a state of instability. It only needs something like this open defiance of your orders to encourage them and they who mock the king openly will stir up a rebellion! If it please Your Majesty, let it be written that they are to be destroyed! This is no time for weakness!"

Ahasuerus was amazed. He rose from the table, walked to the window and stared out upon the view of almond trees blooming bountifully and peacefully. Destruction. Destruction. It was a hideous word. Yet why should he shrink before it? Efficient government required a firm hand. He turned and, still at the window, faced Haman.

"The time for action is come," went on Haman. "The way to insure peace and safety is to wipe out this entire race, leaving none of them alive, preserving no single Jew even as a slave!"

"You speak of the Jews? But these people pay taxes."

"True, and so that Your Majesty and the state shall suffer no loss from the purging of these troublemakers, I myself, out of my own wealth, will repay to the king's treasury forty thousand talents of silver whenever you please. So great is my love for Persia that I would beggar myself to preserve her from internal strife. I will pay this sum willingly, gladly, to rid my beloved country of this menace— so vast is the danger, my lord!"

Ahasuerus was deeply moved. Though he loved Haman, he had never considered him a generous man, and now the fact that Haman had offered this stupendous sum convinced him that there really was danger from the Hebrews, that something was fomenting among them of such a nature that the prime minister was frightened by it.

"I do not doubt the prime minister's patriotism. Whatever the decision, I will not accept this money from you."

"And Your Majesty does not doubt my word in this matter? I assure you from my heart that I have hesitated to speak, but every day it grows worse, and now it has become too serious to delay any longer. The very structure of Persian law is being undermined! We must act!"

"This is a matter to be taken up with the council immediately."

Haman would have preferred that Ahasuerus decide at once, but he had no fear of the council. A group of cringers. They kept what they thought to themselves, and they voted yes or no in accord with the way the king put the proposition to them.

The two men returned to the council chamber immediately. Without preliminaries, Ahasuerus gave Haman permission to address the seven lawyers. The prime minister rose, cleared his throat, stroked his elaborately curled beard.

"My lords," he began, "I have this day set before His Majesty a petition." Haman paused impressively. He was an adept at making these pauses, which added drama and weight to his words. "You all know the wickedness and underhandedness of the Hebrews, their flagrant disrespect for Persian law!"

No one spoke. They were not Amalekites. They neither liked nor disliked the Hebrews. Whatever might happen to the Jews would in no way affect them. They did *not* know that the Israelites were wicked or had shown any disrespect for law. But to contradict Haman would be an invitation to trouble. Harbonah, who was Haman's man, nodded emphatically. The king looked from one to the other of these grave and intelligent faces. Surely, he thought, if Haman had by any possibility been mistaken, some one of them would have arisen to say so.

"You know," went on Haman, looking intently at them all, "that even now this evil nation is stirring up trouble! They are secretive and dangerous! Dangerous, I say, to the well-being of every Persian!"

They had never seen Haman in better style. So convincing was he that they felt uncomfortable, asking themselves if he did have some knowledge which they, had they been properly vigilant, should have had.

"So bold have they become," went on Haman, and he seemed to Ahasuerus the very embodiment of incorruptible statesmanship, "so bold have they become, I say, that now they *publicly* refuse to show proper respect to authority! They are defiant of us! They are stirring up a rebellion. They are traitors! Therefore for the safety of our beloved Persia, I urge you all, if you are loyal Persians, to exterminate this entire race, to have them obliterated, to leave none of them alive, even as captives or slaves!"

This was harsh and stirring language, harshly and stirringly spoken. Menucan gasped and opened his mouth to speak. Some wild thought came to him that he must speak up and say, "No, no, we need not go *that* far!"

But the colorless, aged mouth closed again, for Menucan had seen the eyes of the king and how admiringly they were fixed upon Haman. "What is it to me?" he asked himself. "I am old and tired, tired of altercation." So the moment passed, and Haman was speaking again, resolute, forceful.

"My lords! As I told the king, the time for action has come! Action now is compulsory. We dare not delay. Are we loyal Persians? Then rise and stamp out this menace! Wherever the evil lurks, rout it out, that our king and country may be safe!"

"So be it," said Harbonah quickly. "So be it," said the others.

"My lords," spoke the king, "you have decided. Though I did not doubt the word of my proven friend, I was loth to credit such report. But your agreement prompts me to assume that you yourselves must have made inquiries and these must have satisfied you that the accusation is just."

"As the king has said." Harbonah nodded.

"Of a certainty," put in Carshena.

"Your Majesty," said Haman, "turn this work over to the Amalekites. I promise that it will be thoroughly and speedily accomplished."

"How speedily?"

"In a single day!"

Ahasuerus wanted suddenly to get away from the atmosphere of the council room. At this moment, on a hilltop behind the tabernacle, his priests were preparing for the annual sacrifice of horses to the sun. He was expected to be present during the ceremony. How ancient the custom was he did not know. Many customs of old Persia had been abolished in his reign; the custom, for instance, that no one else could walk upon carpets on which the king had walked. And this custom of sacrificing horses to the sun, seemed to him quite as silly. He rose, hastily took off his silver ring, which was the royal seal, and put it in Haman's hand.

"Here is the seal. Do with these rebels as it seems wise to you. Do not trouble me any more concerning the matter. Our duty is to protect our country, and protection lies in wiping out whatsoever would menace the security and peace of our homes. Now I will leave you. As you know, I am expected at the festival to the sun. After that I am going to the queen."

When the king and his bodyguard had gone, Haman and the seven councillors sank into their chairs.

Shothar gasped. "By the gods! Total destruction!"

Haman was smiling. He was triumphant. Carefully he masked the exuberance he felt. "If you had anything against it, why did you not speak out before the king?"

Harbonah spoke before Shothar could answer. "Who are we to question the sagacity of our illustrious, our noble, our conscientious prime minister? I myself have no liking for Hebrews. I care not whether they live or die."

"So!" said Menucan. "The Amalekites shall at last succeed in destroying the Jews! And when will this slaughter take place?"

"When indeed?" Haman laughed, now in a friendly mood. No one answered. It was as if all of them were afraid to set the fatal date.

"Well," said Haman, the very soul of good nature now, "let us cast Pur."

They smiled with relief, for now the responsibility would not be upon their shoulders. Pur carried the responsibility. Pur was an old Assyrian word meaning "stone." It meant two small squares of stone or ivory with numerals on all six sides. Haman was a superstitious man. Every event of his life was decided by the casting of Pur, or lots.

Now he took two pieces of ivory from his pouch and began shaking them, speaking as he did so. "We shall decide this question by lot. It is now the thirteenth day of the first month. Whatever number comes up, it will be the thirteenth day of that month."

He rolled the squares on the council table. "Twelve!" he grumbled. "A whole year! Twelve months from now. Well, so be it. They will have that much longer to suffer. The thirteenth of Adar is the date. After that, in all the king's dominion, no Hebrew will be alive!"

He went to the door and admitted the six scribes. No sooner were they seated at their portable tables than Haman began dictating.

"Ahasuerus, the great king, to the rulers of the one hundred and twenty-seven provinces from India to Ethiopia, sends this writing.

"Whereas I govern many nations and have obtained dominion of the major part of the habitable earth, I have not been coerced into doing anything that was cruel to my subjects by the power vested in me, but have showed myself lenient, caring for the peace and good order of my people, and seeking that they might enjoy these blessings for all time.

"Whereas I have been kindly informed by Haman, my prime minister and by my council, of the traitorous machinations of the Hebrews; these eight men, by their wisdom, patriotism and sense of justice to my loyal subjects, have voted and set their seals as follows:

"Haman, prudent as just, is first in my esteem. In dignity he is second only to myself. It was he who this day, motivated by his fidelity toward me, informed me that in our midst is this ill-natured nation which holds itself adverse to our laws."

Haman paused. His colleagues removed their rings in readiness to place the seals upon the document. They wanted the thing over with; but Haman relished it so deeply that he wished to prolong it. He took time to put the pieces of ivory carefully back into his pouch. He slowly poured himself a goblet of water from the pitcher on the table. He drank it slowly, sipping it as though it were wine, his head back so that they could see the muscles of his throat as he swallowed. At long last he put the empty goblet on the table and went on dictating.

"The Hebrews hate the monarchy and are of a dangerous, pernicious, disloyal disposition, working the overthrow of the government by secret methods.

"Therefore I give this order: that all Hebrews be destroyed—men, their wives and children—shall be destroyed by my faithful servants, the Amalekites. No Israelite shall be spared. I command that no Persian shall show pity for them or in any way aid them.

"Beginning at sunrise the thirteenth Adar, the Amalekites are to cause to perish Hebrews young and old, little children, infants and women, all are to be killed in this one day of liberation. As reward, the Amalekites are to take the property of the Hebrews.

"This commandment is published thus far in advance in order that every Amalekite be ready for that day. Let none of these people be allowed to live. Let none escape from the country in the interval. Thus may we Persians live the remainder of our lives in that peace which is so dear to us.

"This letter is sent to all my provinces."

When the scribes gave the letters to Haman, he put the king's seal upon them and next to it his own. Then each councillor stepped forward, adding his private seal to those of Haman and Ahasuerus.

Haman was satisfied. When the door had closed upon the scribes, he faced his fellow-councillors. "Our duty to Persia is done," he announced smugly. "I congratulate my lords."

But the councillors did not seem elated. One after another, mumbling excuses, they left the room, and Haman sat alone. So, he mused, it is done. A Hebrew refuses to bow to an Amalekite? Behold the Amalekite's answer! This time next year not one Hebrew would be alive in all Persia. It does not pay to offend an Amalekite.

On the thirteenth day of the twelfth month would take place such a wholesale massacre as had never been seen upon the earth. The purging of Persia was inevitable. The Aryans would be free of the Hebrews. On that document the king, the prime minister and the councillors had placed their seals. That made it unalterable. Even the king could not change the decree now, for the law of the Medes and Persians read:

No decree or statute which the king and his councillors have established can be changed.

Haman was hungry and wanted to eat. He was gleeful and wanted to laugh. So excited was he that as he poured another glass of water, his hand shook. Oh, he thought, this is a night for celebration! What a great and mighty man he was! How cleverly he had managed this affair! King Agag, I have avenged you at last! Every Amalekite in the land would hold jubilee when this decree was known. They would exalt the name of Haman, the prime minister. They would sing his praises in song. They would drink his health in wine and call him their deliverer. They would bless his name in elaborate ceremonies before the altar of their moon-god, Sin.

Even now, in imagination, he could hear the racing hooves of the post horses as they sped in all directions bringing the message. Farmers, plunging their wooden plows into the earth, would learn of it. Shepherds pasturing their flocks in grassy valleys; rug makers, tanners, priests and potentates, gatherers of fruit upon the mountain slopes, all would tremble at the power of the prime minister. And he had once dreamed of wearing the crown? Why, he already wore it! That young fool of a king would do anything he said. Who ruled Persia? Haman the Amalekite.

Meanwhile, having stayed only briefly at the Festival of the Sun, Ahasuerus found surcease from all this talk of danger and rebellion in the arms of the girl he loved. He said nothing to her of what had taken place in the council room. She of the bright eyes and ready smile, she who was so alive, so radiant—what had such unpleasant matters to do with her?

Nothing. Nothing at all.

Esther. Esther. My beloved.

11: The Shadow of Death

NOT UNTIL next day did the Hebrews of Shushan learn of the decree. The news spread like a red flame as throughout the land racing couriers brought copies of the letter to every province. Non-partisan officials read it with horror. Summoned by the trumpets the crowds gathered to listen to the edict, hushed, stunned. Many of these people had Hebrew friends, and now they thought of these friends being slaughtered and themselves forbidden to give aid. They could do nothing. They could not hide a Hebrew in their homes nor during this interval of waiting could they help them to get beyond the borders. Gentiles gazed at one another, troubled and perplexed.

Grimly, in every province, the regional authorities began preparations for the burial of the Jews. This preparation was particularly aggressive in Shushan where the whole enterprise was under the vigilant, merciless gaze of the prime minister.

Everywhere the Amalekites were exultant. At once they went about assembling Scythian daggers, short Persian lances, javelins, knives, clubs, bows, filling slings with stones, and quivers with deadly brass-headed arrows. Priests of Sin called upon their sect to give thanks to the god and praise to the illustrious Haman.

In his palace, seeing none of this and ignorant of what was going on, was Ahasuerus, who had countless other matters to think about. He reasoned that an incipient rebellion, which might have proven dangerous, would be thoroughly wiped out, and the whole matter of punishment to the traitors was in the capable hands of "good, reliable Haman."

Down in the Hebrew quarter men stared at their sons, whose future only yesterday they had been planning. Women gazed about their homes, homes in which they had taken such pride. The entire district swelled with moans and tears. A few more months of life. Wildly they prayed, but they prayed hopelessly. Nothing could save them. Yesterday they had felt safe, safe to make plans for next year or five years or ten years.

When the news reached Mordecai, he was at first only stunned. Then came the realization that he, by not bowing to the prime minister, was to blame for this tragedy.

He took off his rings, his bracelet and his neckchain. He tore his robe in the traditional Hebrew symbol of suffering.

Yesterday he had heard the laughter of children, the tender lullabies of young mothers, the friendly chatter of housewives as they met at the wells or the markets, musicians practicing. Now there was none of that. Now there was only desolation and fear.

He donned sackcloth, took ashes from the fireplace and put them on his head. Then he went out on the streets. In the doorways men sat stupefied. Someone told him that the date for this wholesale execution had been decided by the casting of Pur. He listened jadedly, his body palpitant with dread.

Leaving the quarter, he walked through the streets where the Gentiles lived, shouting the news.

"A nation that has harmed no man is about to be destroyed!" An Amalekite laughed jeeringly. Others looked at Mordecai in pity. But no one stopped him.

"A nation that has harmed no man is about to be destroyed!" He shouted it on his way to the palace, for even now it was unthinkable that he should disobey his king and stay away from the court when he had been commanded to come there daily. Knowing that by law no one in sackcloth could venture inside the gates, he took his place outside them. Here he faced the street. From time to time other Hebrews passed him, men and women, moving aimlessly about. What was the use of working? In less than a year they would all be dead. But some of them, tormented by the unquiet within, were unable to sit still or lie still, even upon the ashes. Weary with dread though they were, action, movement, was life; but they moved silently, like gray ghosts. Sometimes when Mordecai saw them, he saw them blurredly, his dark eyes filled with tears.

In the queen's palace Malme, Acratheus and Sabuchadas looked at each other in horror. "What shall we do?" asked Malme. "Shall we tell the queen?"

"Heaven forbid," muttered Sabuchadas, "that I should be the one to bring her such news! Poor lady, always so gentle, so joyous, so considerate, so sweet. It will break her heart. Acratheus, you are the head of the house. It is for you to tell her."

"No, no. Not yet—not yet. She has been so happy this morning. I heard her singing. Never has her voice sounded so rich and lovely. It was a joy to listen."

Malme sighed. "As I massaged her, she kept making little jokes with me. As full as is the sun of light, so full of gladness is she. How could he have done a thing like this? He is a good man, a kind man. How could he have done this?"

"Crafty old Haman. Haman rules him. Haman can do no wrong."

"It makes me afraid. It makes me afraid."

"We have nothing to fear."

"How do you know we have not? If such a thing can be done to one people, is anyone safe? And how shall I speak to her naturally when she calls me? How can I meet her eyes? I am confused. I—oh! That is her bell."

Malme hastened away in answer to the queen's summons. "I am ready to put on my robe now," said Esther lightly. "Something gay today. What a day it is! The air is so cool and the sun so bright. Everything seems to sparkle in the sunlight." She sighed blissfully. "How good everyone has been to me here!"

"The—pink robe?"

"Yes, and my turquoise jewelry. Why do you stare so stupidly? Is something wrong?"

"No. No, nothing, Your Majesty."

"Is it some trouble that has come upon you?"

"No trouble has come upon me."

"Then how can you look so depressed on a day like this?" Esther opened a large ebony box and took out a pair of splendid earrings. "I have so much to give. Take them. Wear them in health."

"I thank Your Majesty. An old face like mine does no credit to such gems. But all the same, I thank you. The pink robe, you said, and the—er—green sandals?"

"Green sandals? With a pink robe and turquoise jewelry? Now I know there is something the matter when you, of all people, suggest a thing like that." She laid an affectionate hand on Malme's wrist. "Let me help you."

"There is nothing wrong with me." Malme brought the pink robe and put it on her mistress. Then she brought the little pink sandals and knelt to put them on Esther's feet. As soon as possible she left the room.

When it came time for Mordecai to arrive, Esther went to the window and stood watching for him.

But his usual place was empty. Was he ill? What else could keep him away? Worried now, she summoned Acratheus.

"My uncle is late today."

Acratheus avoided her eyes. She noticed how mournful he looked. He stood there awkwardly, and she got the impression that he was carefully considering every word he spoke.

"No, he is there, but today he stands outside the gate and Your Majesty cannot see him from the window."

"Why does he stand outside?"

"Because it is not lawful for anyone to enter within the gate in mourning attire."

"Mourning! Mordecai in mourning? Why? Why?"

"I—cannot say. I only know that I caught a glimpse of him and he is in sackcloth."

"Now, this is strange. Go to him. Go to him at once. Tell him to put away his mourning and take his place inside the gates."

"I will tell him, Your Majesty."

A few minutes later he was back. "Well?" she asked. "Well, speak! What baleful thing has befallen my uncle? Why does he wear sackcloth?"

"He bids me tell Your Highness that he cannot put off his sackcloth because—because the sad occasion which forces him to wear it has not ceased."

"Sad occasion? What sad occasion?"

Again Acratheus avoided her eyes. "I did not ask him," he replied evasively.

"Now go back and do so. Tell him I must know what has befallen him. Ask him why he is in mourning and what is this sad occasion."

"Must I go? I have an appointment to see an upholsterer."

"I care nothing about your appointment."

Acratheus bowed and withdrew. Esther sat, frowning. She gazed down at her frothy pink robe, at the ringed hands clasped so tightly.

Why should she be dressed like this when Mordecai was in mourning? What was keeping Acratheus so long? She felt suddenly cold, shivered a little and reached for a filmy shawl which hung from the back of the chair. Then a few minutes later she was too hot and flung it aside impatiently. Mordecai was a fastidious man. It was not his way to wear sackcloth except for some valid reason.

"At last!" she exclaimed as Acratheus entered.

"Your Majesty, the reason your uncle is in mourning is because—because of a decree which has gone out from the king."

"What has the king's decree to do with my uncle?"

There was no way to ease the blow. Acratheus spoke bluntly.

"The decree is this, that on the thirteenth day of Adar every Jew in Persia, even the little babies, must be slaughtered!"

She gasped. She clutched the side of her chair, feeling dizzy, sick and faint. She murmured, "No, no," like a person in a delirium.

"It cannot be," she muttered at last. "My uncle must be mistaken. It cannot be."

Acratheus held out the paper. "Here is a copy of the decree.

Mordecai gave it to me. He copied it himself. He asks that you read it."

She read it, and when she had read it a second time, she looked up helplessly at Acratheus. "There is a eunuch in service for the king whom His Majesty sends to me with messages and gifts. Find him and bring him here."

It was half an hour before Hatach arrived. Like all those who served Esther, he loved her.

She spoke calmly. "Hatach, I have just received a copy of a decree to annihilate the Jews. I thought that you, being in attendance at the king's palace, might know how this atrocious thing came about."

"Your Highness, we know few of the details. It is known, however, that Haman persuaded the king to this measure, and that Haman decided the date. As everyone knows, he is superstitious, and the date for the massacre was determined by his casting of Pur."

"And where was the king at this time?"

"It took place while he was here with you. He had put the matter entirely in the prime minister's hands. I swear that is the extent of my knowledge in the matter."

"That is all, Hatach. Thank you."

When Hatach had gone, she faced Acratheus. "Did—did my uncle tell you what I am to do?"

"I did not tell Your Majesty before, because you cannot do what he asks."

"Tell me what he said."

"He asks that as soon as possible Your Majesty petition the king about the matter. Mordecai said, 'Tell her not to think it a dishonorable thing now for her to put on humble dress. The safety of her people is in her hands. Tell her I beg of her to see the king and make complaint as to this ruination of the Jews. She must understand that it is Haman, not something her people have done, that has brought this about.' "

"He—asks me to go—to the king?"

"But Your Majesty cannot do it! You must not do it! You have your own life to think of, and if not your life, your future. Remember Vashti!"

Vashti. Yes. He had put Vashti aside because she had disobeyed him, because she had broken a law. And he had loved Vashti. She remembered, too, the profound earnestness in his voice when shortly after their marriage, he had said, "You will never test my love, Esther. Promise me that you will never break a law!" And she had answered, "I promise."

She recalled, too, her husband's terrible temper. She imagined the fury of his anger unleashed upon herself. No. She dared not do this. She turned her head in the direction of Vashti's distant house. Could she invite a similar fate? Or perhaps worse? By this act she ran the risk of forfeiting his love, which was dearer to her than life itself. She knew that he loved her, but also she knew his nature. He was capable of cutting out his own heart, burning out his own eyes, if by doing so he could uphold the law of Persia. It had caused him pain to divorce Vashti, yet he had done it.

"Go back to my uncle," she said. "Say that by law the queen cannot approach the king unless he summons her. Make Mordecai understand that anyone who goes to the king without being called is slain on the spot unless—that is, if the king is willing to save anyone, he holds out the golden scepter to him, then that person is pardoned. Explain to Mordecai that what he asks is impossible. I dare not do it. I beg him to remember Vashti."

"I will make it clear that in doing what he asks, you risk your life, and that for less than such a presumptuous act, Vashti was divorced. I will do my best to convince your uncle that, to the king, nothing is so reprehensible as for anyone, but especially you, to break the law."

Alone, Esther read the barbarous decree several times. Each reading increased her horror and her fear. She fought off faintness. She rose, and was forced to cling to the chair for support. Afraid of falling, she sat down again. Her body felt so limp and weak that it seemed as if some unseen power were mercilessly draining it of life.

How could this monstrous thing have happened and why? She saw Haman, not as a cruel and rapacious person, but as evil incarnate. How could evil have such power? Evil in the council chamber. Evil walking the earth, strutting, gloating. Evil demanding that everyone bow down to it and fear it and cringe before it.

"God help me!" she cried. "Help us all!"

Then Acratheus was in the room. His face was white, his voice was tense.

"Your uncle says you must act boldly!"

She looked at him with fixed, despairing eyes. "Did you explain about the law and how it is that I cannot go to the king unless His Majesty summons me?"

"I told him that. He bade me tell Your Majesty that you must not only make every attempt to save yourself, but to save your people. His exact words were, 'Tell the queen that she need not think that because she is in the king's house she will escape any more than the rest of us. Who knows whether Esther has not been brought to her present position for just such a time as this?' "

She sat looking at the floor, trying to formulate some plan. Acratheus waited, his eyes pityingly upon her. At last she raised her head.

"Send Malme to me. Then return to Mordecai. Tell him it is my desire that he go to the Hebrew section and gather our people in a group. He is to tell them that they are to fast for three days. I will do the same. Say to Mordecai that even though it be against the law, and even though I die for it, I will go to the king. Now, it may be that, instead of risking my life by going to the king, he will come to me. So when you have spoken to my uncle, go to the king's palace. Request an audience as one who comes from me. If you are permitted to see His Majesty, beseech him to come to me as soon as possible."

Acratheus bowed and left. In the hall he met Malme, whose position required her to stay near the queen.

"She wants you," said Acratheus. Malme entered the queen's room.

"I want neither food nor drink for three days," announced Esther.

"But —"

"And find me a sackcloth robe. One of the maids must have one."

"Persia's queen in sackcloth? Oh, that would never do!"

Esther spoke firmly. "I will have no ornaments, no perfume, no sandals. I am in mourning. Go and get the robe."

Malme left, fuming. "The queen of Persia in sackcloth!"

Meanwhile, Acratheus had delivered Esther's message to Mordecai and then hastened up the steps to the royal palace. In a wide reception hall every chair was occupied by people awaiting an audience. Soldiers stood at intervals, and at one side of a tall closed door sat a scribe at a marble table.

Beyond those stately doors the king sat with his ministers, surrounded by his ten axemen. For two nights he had not slept. Another border incident had assumed alarming proportions and the country was on the brink of war.

How to avoid it? Should they send restitution for the damage done? If so, how much? And would such an act be interpreted as weakness? Should they send ambassadors to Greece to arbitrate the matter? If so, how many and whom? A thousand queries had arisen. Every moment was precious.

As Acratheus approached the doortender, the man looked up at him. "You come from the queen?"

"I do. I beg you to ask His Majesty to see me. It is a matter of grave importance."

"Is the queen ill?"

"No, but she wishes to see the king at once."

The doorkeeper shook his head. "If she is not ill, then I dare not interrupt His Majesty. And even if she were, I would not do it. I have been given orders that until he so signifies, he is not to be disturbed—on any matter."

"Is there any use for me to wait?"

"No use. All day and well into the night the conferences go on. I do not know what it is, but they are all under some terrific strain. To interrupt the king now—it would be equal to committing suicide."

There was nothing for Acratheus to do but return to Esther and tell her this news. What a change he found in her! She had stripped herself of ornaments. Her little feet were bare. All cosmetics had been washed from her face, and she wore a shapeless sackcloth robe. He knew that in times of grief it was the custom of her people to go barefooted and wear such unbecoming garments, and his natural tact prevented him from making any comment.

Esther received the news silently. Then, after a time she looked up at him, saying, "A letter! You will take a letter to him. I will write it myself." But her hand trembled. Finally she put down the pen and said piteously, more to herself than to him, "Perhaps it is better not to write it, for I could not explain why it is so imperative that I see him. No, I will wait, for what

I have to say should only be said when we two are face to face."

There was in her the hope that perhaps the king might come to her tonight. Or tomorrow. She would wait for that. Meanwhile, she wanted to be alone, to prepare herself, to plan. With a wave of her hand she dismissed Acratheus and sat thinking what she would do if the king did not come before the end of her three-day fast.

Unable to remain inactive, she went out into the courtyard and like a melancholy gray wraith walked with downcast head among the trees. At first her mind was only with Mordecai and her people. She felt their tears within her own body. She knew that even if by some miracle she could escape the slaughter, if all her people were killed, she would never find happiness in the king's arms again.

She asked herself how Ahasuerus could have permitted a thing like this to happen, and she realized more clearly than ever now the extent of Haman's power over him. Surely, Ahasuerus could not have dictated that letter, even though it bore his seal. She could not believe that he would doom babies, children and women. Persian law demanded the death penalty for traitors, but only a diabolical mind could have included infants in that category. The whole thing was unlike her husband. Only an incarnate fiend could have written that decree. And what of the councillors? What manner of men were they?

So, as she walked, she tried to reason the problem out. It was impossible to come to any conclusion other than that the king and his councillors were all tools of Haman, and Haman was a monster. But how was she to unmask him?

The lives of thousands of people were in her hands. And what was ahead of her but defeat, divorce, even death?

She realized that the sun was setting. A red burst of light showered the treetops and the distant hills. Ahasuerus might come to her at any moment. Speaking silently, she faced the direction of his palace. "Ahasuerus! Come to me! Come! You must hear me calling! You must feel my need of you, whether you are in the throne room or the council chamber!" But then the thought came that it might be better if he did not come. It was better to think of some plan whereby she could bring both the king and Haman here.

Yes! Confront both of them together in her own home. Then she could accuse Haman to his face, accuse him openly before the king. And then? Would Ahasuerus defend Haman against her? Were they both so involved in this heinous thing that the king, in defending Haman, would defend himself? If that were true, how could she even let him touch her hand again?

But these questions were at present unanswerable. Her prime concern was how she was to get them both here at the same time. A dinner. Tell Ahasuerus that she wished to honor his favorite by having them both to dinner with her. Such a move on her part would put Haman off his guard.

First, she would go to the king. If he held out his golden scepter to her, if the axemen did not kill her, this would be proof that Ahasuerus loved her even more deeply than he had loved Vashti. If it happened in this way, then she would invite the king and Haman to a dinner, saying that she wished to honor the prime minister. Then she would wait her time, and when Haman was relaxed and his suspicions were quiescent, she would accuse him. And *then* what? What would be the king's reaction?

Would he permit her to be killed with her people? Would he despise her because she was a Jewess, one of that race against which his mind had already been poisoned?

To go to the king when he had not summoned her! At the mere thought of it her knees went weak, and lest she fall in a heap on the ground, she staggered to a bench. She loved Ahasuerus, and now she risked forfeiting his love, that love which was dearer to her than life.

Dusk came, and the night chill. She moved back to the palace, up the stairs and into her room. There she stood, not at a window overlooking the public court, but at a window which overlooked the palace grounds.

Even in the waning light, magnificence was everywhere. Here was the beauty and the glory and the luxury that was Persia. She had always been warmly appreciative of the loveliness of the view from this window, but now she felt remote from it all, out of place here, alone—and *little*.

She walked to a window on the left where she could look down upon the city, and where, one day pointing to the south, Malme had indicated the Hebrew quarter. She belonged with them. True, they were austere and aloof from the Gentiles, but they obeyed the laws, paid their taxes, and were loyal to the government. The fact that so many of them remained in the king's dominions when they were free to return to Jerusalem proved their love for this country.

Esther sighed, shook her head, and walking to the bed, lay upon it wearily. She stretched out on her back, staring into space, aware of a pain in her head. Malme came in, bringing two lamps.

"Your Majesty is still not hungry?"

Hungry—yes. Perhaps eating would relieve the headache. She was unbearably hungry. But she said no, that she would not break her fast, and Malme was to consider herself relieved from duty for the rest of the night.

"Your Majesty does not want me to help you undress? Come, lady, let me remove from you that ugly, unbecoming robe."

"No. Go away. Go away."

Malme went out, closing the door softly behind her, and Esther was alone again. She began to weep, and as she wept she kept saying to herself, "This is the time to be brave. Be brave. Be strong." But she was neither brave nor strong, and ashamed of her weakness. The thought of food kept coming to her—a bit of water, a sip of goat's milk to wet her throat. But she resisted the urge to call for it, and turned her thought to Mordecai, wondering what he was doing.

Mordecai had gone up and down the streets of the Hebrew quarter summoning the people to the small synagogue. They did not ask why. They came. Women carrying infants or holding young children by the hand; young girls and boys; couples just married; the middle-aged and the old. Not now did the men and women follow the usual custom of separating at the door. Families clung together as though loth to part even for a brief interval, because now they had so little time left to be together.

When they were all gathered within the synagogue, Mordecai mounted the lectern and faced them. They looked up helplessly at the tall, spare man in sackcloth. Except for a single nervous cough from somewhere in the rear, there was no sound.

"Why have I called you here and without invitation from the elders and chief priests dared to mount your lectern? It is because I have something to say which comes from the queen."

The queen! Sending a message to them? A glimmer of interest showed in the dull eyes.

"Not long ago I came to Shushan. My name is Mordecai ben Jair, of the tribe of Benjamin. Since coming here I have been each day in the court of the king, and now I bring a message from the queen."

One of the priests spoke up. "The queen! Surely, like the king, she despises us."

"Not so, friend. The queen loves you, for she is a Hebrew."

"What? The queen?"

Now a flicker of hope leapt into eyes bloodshot and swollen with weeping. The queen a Hebrew? Could it be that their merciful God in His love had placed in the palace a deliverer, a savior—and was that savior to be a woman? Their wits were too dulled by anguish to wonder why the queen should have communicated with this newcomer.

"Your queen commands," Mordecai continued, "that you fast for the next three days, even as she will do. She asks that we all pray together, that we ask our God not to forget His people at this time when they are threatened with destruction. And as we pray, let us have faith. Even in this trial, let us cling fast to our faith! How often in the past has God forgiven us and provided for us? He alone can deliver us from this destruction which has been decreed against us! We know that everyone of us is a loyal Persian and that we are grateful for the opportunities and freedom we have found here. We know that we have not been disloyal nor have we stirred up any trouble against our government. We have not offended in any way, yet we are to be slain, forbidden even the right of self-defense. And now I confess to you all that I am to blame for it!"

They gasped.

"How can this be?" asked an aged elder. "You wear the turban of a scribe. You appear to be a law-abiding citizen."

"I refused to worship the prime minister. I refused to bow down to him. And because of his anger at me, he has conceived this calamity upon us all—upon us, who have never transgressed any law of the land!"

"Woe! Woe! Alas! Alas!" they moaned in unison.

One of the rabbis spoke up. "We do not blame you for what has happened. We all know how hard a thing it is to bow to an Amalekite. What has been done, is done. Now let us pray. That is all we can do. Let us ask God to deliver us, to free not only ourselves but every Israelite in the land from this calamity."

So the multitude prayed, each one silently and in his own fashion.

At that identical moment Esther was praying, too. For three days at intervals she prayed. For three days she tasted nothing but water. She saw no one but Malme.

Finally, on the night of the third day, she declared quietly that tomorrow she would go to the king. Had she announced that she intended to jump off a cliff, Malme could not have been more astounded. She stared at Esther incredulously.

"Are you mad? Yes, you are mad to go to him when he has not summoned you. This foolish fast has made you light-headed."

"I am going to the king."

"You cannot. You know the law. Oh, forgive me for speaking so, but I have grown to love you! I cannot bear the thought of anything happening to you. Do not do this, do not! It is suicidal. It—"

"I shall go to him tomorrow. I shall wear my most becoming robe, my jewels. You will wash my hair, bathe me and anoint me."

"You expect me to dress you for your death or—or your—divorce? Oh, listen to reason!"

"I must do this. It is the only way to save my people."

"I beg you to think what is at stake!"

"Everything is at stake. Everything. Oh, be still. Be still. I am in no mood for talking. Bring forth the robes and let me choose." Her eyes filled with tears. She dashed them away, telling herself sternly that this was no time for tears. "No, no, that is not good enough," she said, as Malme brought forth the pink robe, the robe that was so girlish and delicate and gay.

Baffled and tormented she sat, feverishly waving aside one robe after another. Malme lit the lamps, and the inspection of the queen's wardrobe began again.

"What would any woman want with so many?" Esther muttered wearily. "Take that green one for yourself, and the pale-blue one, and the red. Who knows? I may never wear any of them again."

Am I seeing those robes for the last time? Even if he permits me to go on living, will I come back to this room? All those robes.

Why were they chosen but to please her husband? Would she ever please him again? Would she ever again feel his arms about her and his kisses on her mouth? Uncertainties. Everything was uncertain. Only three days ago she had been secure and certain, certain of his love, certain of happiness, certain of safety, certain of life. Now there was nothing but torment and fear, nothing but the shadow of death.

She recalled a song, a song composed long ago by her ancestor's song maker—David, the Bethlemite. Part of the song repeated itself again and again in her mind, *Though I walk through the valley of the shadow of death, I will fear no evil, for thou art with me—*

It gave her no comfort. It was only words. What was she doing, walking through the valley of the shadow of death in this green and glowing and lovely world? This world where the sun was tranquilly shining and the wheat was growing? Her heart was pounding now so that she could scarcely breathe.

Malme's eyes were sullen as she continued to bring out gown after gown. At last Esther chose one. It was a diaphanous black gown with a long train, low cut at the throat. Its lines were slim and clinging. There was a slit up the front, and about the hem and armholes were borders of gold embroidery. She chose gold sandals, gold bracelets and heavy earrings that were like disks. She had worn the robe once and felt sophisticated in it. She knew that it made her seem taller and made her skin seem more fair. Ahasuerus had never seen her in it.

In the morning she broke her fast with a goblet of goat's milk. Then she permitted Malme to bathe her and scent her body with costly oil imported from Araby. She put on her black robe and noted that the slit in the center of the skirt revealed her lovely legs to above the knees. Next she sat before a mirror as with expert hands Malme applied the cosmetics.

"Outline my brows like the black wings of birds in flight, with an upward sweep—Paint my mouth redder—" She was trying to make her voice sound natural and calm. "So, now. More kohL"

Malme burst into sudden tears. "Do you realize that I may be dressing you for your death? Oh, do not do this unlawful thingl"

"My bracelets—now my rings and my heaviest gold necklace—now the earrings. Stop trembling so. Go tell Acratheus that I want red roses out of the garden to carry in my arms, long stemmed, and with the thorns removed."

When Malme had gone, Esther began to choose the headdress she would wear. A simple gold band? A diadem of jewels? The crown? Oh, if only her body would stop quivering so! If only this dizziness would go!

As if challenging the dizziness, she rose and stood before the mirror. Yes, in this gown she looked extremely tall. With its long, fan-shaped train and its heavy edging of gold, it was truly a court gown. The train spread out behind her in a wide circle. It was the weight of the train which skillfully pulled back the opening in the front, so that the tapering white beauty of her legs showed in striking contrast against the dull black veiling of the robe itself.

She considered wearing the crown, but it was heavy and her head ached. No, not the crown. Her hair—long, lustrous and sweetly scented, with a slight natural wave, was in itself her most enticing ornament. Ahasuerus had always said that he loved her hair.

Dizzy, head aching, inwardly trembling, Esther said to her reflection in the mirror that she could not do this thing. Cold compresses had taken the redness and swelling from her eyelids but she looked tired and her steps were unsteady. The impulse came to her to postpone this meeting—just one day, just one more day.

Though I walk through the valley of the shadow of death, I will fear no evil, for thou—art with me—

They were like words spoken from out a troubled sleep. She stood, frozen there, imagining the king when he saw her. She clutched the back of the chair for support.

Malme entered carrying a sheaf of roses. Behind her came another maid whose duty it would be to pick up the towels, refill the vials of perfume, neatly rearrange the jewels in their cases.

"You are still determined to do this!" sobbed Malme. "And you know full well what it means! I had hoped that at the last minute you would change your mind. I had hoped that you would see reason."

The fact that Malme was speaking to her, not as to a queen but to an unreasonable child, only endeared her to Esther.

The queen spoke gently. "You—you will go with me."

"I? I have no wish to see you slain. I—"

"You will go with me. Let me lean upon your arm. I—I feel too weak to walk alone. And you—" she spoke to the maid, "the train is heavy. Its weight seems to be holding me back. Pick up my train and carry it."

The maid took up the train, holding it with the tips of her fingers. One arm filled with red roses, the other tucked into Malme's, the queen of Persia left the room, walked down the stairs, passed through the length of the reception hall, and finally came to Acratheus and Sabuchadas who, grim-faced, were tensely waiting to open the door.

"Your Majesty," Acratheus pleaded desperately, "I beseech you, turn back! Do not do this foolhardy, unlawful thing!"

Her eyes met his, her voice rang out with all the commanding tones of a queen. "Open the door and precede me, both of you. I shall go to the king. I know it is not according to law, and if I perish, I perish!"

Into the dazzling sunlight of the public court they went, Sabuchadas calling out, "Make way for the queen of Persia!"

The people fell to their knees. With her four attendants, looking neither to left nor right, the queen ascended the stairs to the king's palace.

Finally they were walking toward the closed door, through the anteroom which was more crowded than ever now, for the king had given no audiences for a week.

The doorkeeper gasped and sprang to his feet. The queen! How dared she do a thing like this? But he knelt, and then rose without being told to do so.

"Her Majesty wishes?" he asked in a tone of proper deference.

"To see the king at once."

"Your Majesty knows the law. Has Her Highness been summoned? I have no such notification here. An oversight, perhaps?"

"It is no oversight. I have not been summoned."

He blinked. "Then, Your Majesty, I cannot, I dare not open that door. My lord the king has said that he is to be disturbed by no one—no one! He is in a black mood. He—"

"Open that door!"

He shook his head. "I am sorry, Your Majesty. I do not mean to be insolent, but I am under command of the king and not the queen. The king," he added meaningly, "tolerates no disobedience—from anyone."

She turned to Acratheus and Sabuchadas. "You are my servants. You obey me. Now I command you—*open that door!*"

12: A Surprise for Haman

LIGHT from two of the long windows seemed to focus upon the king, glinting upon the jewels in his crown and robe. This robe, with winglike, open sleeves, was woven of gold threads upon which jewels of every color had been strung. The sheen of the gold and the gleam of the precious gems made him seem to be garbed in multi-hued light.

He was in the midst of a sentence when the tall doors at the far end of the throne room were flung open. All talk ceased. Ahasuerus leaned forward, furious at the interruption. Who dared intrude at this time?

And there in the doorway was Esther leaning upon the arm of a plain, middle-aged woman while a squat little maid held up her long train with the tips of her trembling fingers.

The king was speechless. Thoughts raced rapidly through his head. Esther! How could she presume to do such a thing? How could she break a law and force him into so hideous a position? Esther, who had always been so docile!

At first, Esther's face flushed a deep red, but as she advanced the flush subsided and her face grew pallid, her eyes abnormally bright. Malme felt her sway. The queen made a valiant effort to keep smiling, but to her heightened imagination, the light, glinting upon the axes, made them seem enormous, threatening. She had the feeling that they were moving closer to her, silent, inescapable. The sun's beams, scintillating upon the king's robe, gave him the appearance of an unearthly being enveloped in flame.

She saw his eyes, glaring at her, alien, harsh. She saw Haman standing there, and his dark, narrow, beaky face assumed the grotesque characteristics of a vulture. For a few minutes everything, every color, every face, every object, was enlarged and intensified. Then suddenly everything blurred and it was as if the whole room started spinning—one huge, whirling mass of colors and faces. She must not spin with it. She must not scream. She must not fall.

Midway to the throne she sank to the floor in a heap. Ahasuerus gave a sharp cry, ran to her, lifted her unconscious body in his arms and laid it tenderly upon a divan. Forgotten now was his rage at what she had done, forgotten were his councillors, the scribes, the axemen.

Esther. Was she dead? Love must have brought her here. Love had made her risk her life just to see him. All these weeks he had neglected her. How beautiful she was! She must not die. He held her in his arms, kissing her face and throat. "Esther! Esther, beloved! Look at me. Speak to me. No, no, my love, don't be afraid!"

Her eyelids fluttered, lifted. She stared at him in fear, gave a long moan and closed her eyes again.

"Esther," he pleaded tenderly, "do not be afraid. Open your eyes. Smile, my dear one. Do not expect punishment because you came as you did, without being called."

She opened her eyes and stared at him, but still she said nothing, and to make his forgiveness official, he reached for his scepter, and smiling at her reassuringly, touched her shoulder with it. The axemen returned to their accustomed places about the throne. Malme and the maid drew close together. The councillors leaned forward, seemingly frozen. Esther sat up, gazing into the eyes of the man she loved. She was not to be killed. She was not to be divorced. She was still queen of Persia.

"My lord the king," she said in a faint voice, "I thank you for your leniency. I confess I have done a wrong thing, a punishable thing."

"It is all forgiven," he assured her tenderly.

In her weakness, she was lovely to him. Her very presence brought a joyous excitement. A moment before he had been tired with the strain of the past weeks, but now he felt full of vigor again, yet he was concerned because of the deep, deep suffering in her eyes.

Weak and shaken though she was, Esther knew that this was a time for discretion. Ahasuerus had forgiven her for coming. She was not to die at the hands of those scowling axemen. That much was sure; but now she must move warily. Her eyes rested upon Haman. He stood there, obviously admiring her beauty, smiling as though he took pleasure in beholding her.

She saw the forgiving smiles on the faces of the councillors, for how could these sycophants frown when the king had forgiven? The whole atmosphere of the room had suddenly changed. She felt a cool, refreshing breeze from a nearby window. "Now I have nothing to fear," she said to herself. But still her heart was fluttering so wildly that she could scarcely breathe or speak. Again her eyes met those of the king.

"Do not tremble so, my love," he said softly. "Be at ease now and tell me why you have come. Do not be distressed. Speak plainly. Why have you done this? Is it some burden that you carry which is in my power to lighten?"

"My lord, indeed I am unnerved. When I saw you sitting there, so great, so powerful, so wondrously handsome—oh, I know not why, but it seemed as though all the life went out of me."

"There is pain in your eyes, Esther. Your smile is forced. Now then, do not be anxious about anything. Tell me what you wish, for should the occasion require it, I am ready to grant you half of my kingdom!"

"Yet it is so small a thing that I require of my lord. It is this. If it seem good to the king, tomorrow evening let him sup with me, and if I may be permitted to honor the friend whom the king honors, then let Lord Haman also be my guest. And when you are both come, then—then I will present my petition to the king."

So, thought Ahasuerus, that is all it is! She has been lonely. She wishes to show me honor by honoring my friend. That is sweet, that is touching.

Haman was astonished. Everyone knew that only close masculine relatives of the king and queen could sit at table in the queen's palace. Esther's request plus the king's agreement to it, would prove to the world how high he stood in the estimation of the king. Even the queen paid homage to Haman! And how enchanting she was! In his outrageous vanity, he asked himself: could it be that the queen who heretofore had seemed to dislike him, could it be that that apparent dislike had been only a mask to cover a secret love? Was he so attractive to women that even the queen—?

"Your request is granted, Esther," Ahasuerus was saying.

"I thank Your Majesty. I crave forgiveness for this intrusion. I—I shall await eagerly the time when you and your friend will sit with me at my table."

She spoke a trifle breathlessly and her eyes were so wide, so childlike, that Ahasuerus had to struggle with himself not to take her in his arms. She bowed to him and then bowed graciously to the councillors, who had risen and were also bowing. Meeting the eyes of Haman, she shuddered to find him smiling at her with a boldness and yet a furtiveness that was so repulsive to her that she turned away quickly, not taking Malme's arm nor motioning to the maid to pick up her train.

When they had returned to her own apartment, Acratheus breathed a huge sigh of relief. Malme's eyes were bright.

"It was a terrible moment," she declared. "When that door opened, when he saw her—oh, may I never again have a moment like that!"

All weakness had departed from Esther now. She was resolute and calm as she began to speak to Acratheus about tomorrow night's dinner.

"Haman?" he asked. "Coming here? Your Highness will sit at meat—with Haman?"

She gave no explanation and went on planning the banquet, choosing every dish that her husband liked. She decided upon soft music—lutists and harpists—hidden behind a curtain. They were to play only soothing melodies. She chose the incense to be burned in the braziers, something spicy yet sweet. She wanted many lights.

The prime minister had never been so happy as he was that day. He scarcely heard what his colleagues were saying. He could hardly wait to tell his family and his friends of this new honor. He planned how he would tell it, with significant winks and shrugs and sly innuendoes. But when, on leaving the palace, he saw Mordecai, still unbowing, his vanity was instantly deflated.

He gritted his teeth savagely. Everyone honored him—his king, the queen, his friends, the people, everyone—except this Hebrew!

Reaching his home, he told his wife and his sons about the queen's invitation. He sent messengers to his friends, summoning them to his house so that he could boast before a larger audience of the honor that had been paid to him. His friends were fawning and congratulatory. When they had gone and he was alone with his aging wife, he was still in a restless, talkative mood.

"Tomorrow I sup with the queen. She braved punishment to come into the throne room and deliver the invitation herself. The king and I! Never before has Esther the queen let any man except the king come to a banquet which she has served. Yet what does this avail me? Everyone pays honor to me except this one man. Oh, with my own hands I would like to break the fellow's neck! There he stands, insolent and proud. And I shall have to be humiliated like this for months."

"Why?" asked his wife shrewdly.

"Eh?"

"Why? Why must you endure this insult for months?"

He gazed at her sharply, reading her meaning. His voice became oily again. "Why, indeed?" he asked smoothly.

"Why should you not punish this man yourself? Why wait for the time of the Hebrews' execution? Why not make that man a public example? Have a gallows constructed in the front court. Have it made fifty cubits high. Have it done tonight. In the morning it could be ready. Then you could go to the king and ask permission to hang this man ahead of the others. What will one Jew less matter to the king? Then, when this is done, you can go merrily to the queen's banquet and there will be nothing to mar my lord's pleasure."

"You are right. Send for the carpenters."

When the laborers came he told them that he wanted a gallows put in the exact center of his front court. It must be ready by morning and it must be fifty cubits high.

"It shall be done, my lord," answered the chief carpenter. "But—er—did I understand the prime minister to say fifty cubits?"

"Fifty cubits, no less. I want this man who is to hang from it to dangle high in the air so that all the people will see him."

All night by the flares of many torches the carpenters worked. Though it kept the prime minister awake, the sound was sweet in his ears. In the morning before leaving for the palace he went into his court and stood looking with untold satisfaction upon that tall, fine gallows. He imagined Mordecai hanging from it. Oh, that Hebrew would bow now! He would cringe and grovel, pleading for mercy.

Pleased with himself and his world, richly garbed as usual, Haman proceeded to the palace. Today he had chosen glittery garments, garments which made him feel younger. But now he was not satisfied even by the honor the queen had paid him yesterday. He wanted more.

The highest honor, an honor greater than even the privilege of dining with the queen, was this: The king permitted a man to dress in his own jeweled purple robe and ride his own horse through the streets, with the king's ring on his finger and one of the king's diadems upon his head. Some noble must lead the way, calling out that this man was being honored by the king. This signified that the man had rendered the king and the country some great service.

Haman's ambition was boundless. Now he coveted that honor. But first he must ask permission to hang a man. He reasoned that this was an excellent time to make the request, for yesterday, after the queen had left, a way had been found to avert the threatened war. This meant that after the fearful pressure of the past weeks, His Majesty would have slept well and would be in a relaxed and amiable mood. So Haman came to the palace unusually early, hoping to have a word with the king before the councillors arrived upon the little matter of a hanging.

But Ahasuerus had not slept at all. Now that the strain was over he had returned to his room thinking longingly of rest, yet once in bed, he tossed wakefully. His mind kept reverting to the events of the day. He remembered how skillfully he had solved the problem of impending war, and felt pleased with himself. He recalled the dramatic entrance of the queen, thought of her beauty, of her dread, of the pain in her eyes, and wondered what the request might be which she would ask of him at the approaching banquet for three.

Finally, growing more wakeful and knowing that many duties had been necessarily neglected all this time, he called his scribes.

"Why should I waste time lying idly in bed when I cannot sleep? Now then, read the records of the past month so that I may acquaint myself with any unfinished business which should be taken up on the morrow. Better that I spend these hours in doing something that will be of benefit to the kingdom. Proceed."

The chief scribe read the chronicles. From time to time as the reader paused for breath, Ahasuerus would smile and say, "Well, *that* matter has been taken care of"—"Yes, we have disposed of *that* problem."

Outside, a full moon silvered the leaves of the olives trees and illumined every path. The radiant silence beyond the opened windows was broken now and then by a nightingale's song. As the scribe's voice went on and on in a monotonous drone, Ahasuerus turned his eyes toward the window and lost himself in the beauty of the night, its serenity and orderliness.

Smiling appreciatively at the beauty of the world and the languorous magic of the night, he settled back more comfortably in his chair. Finally he watched the dark receding; at first faintly and furtively, a wan gray light appeared in the east. As the scribe continued to read, the king closed his eyes. Then suddenly the eyes opened. He leaned forward.

"What? Read that again!"

The scribe had reached that portion of the record which dealt with the attempt on the king's life by Bigthan and Teresh.

"Mordecai!" exclaimed Ahasuerus. "And he has been in the court all this time? He saved my life and I have not given him any reward? Surely, I have not overlooked a thing like that! Read on. What honor has been given to him?"

"Your Majesty, there was nothing done for him."

"Now I have been most remiss. I shall attend to it the first thing in the morning. But it is morning now. You may go, all of you."

When the men had left, Ahasuerus recalled various other gifts he had given as rewards for outstanding service. One man had received the governorship of a province. Another had received a valuable present. But Mordecai had received no reward at all. And Mordecai had saved his life! What recompense was suitable for such a service as this?

As he breakfasted, Ahasuerus continued to ponder the matter, but he could reach no conclusion regarding it.

"Is anyone in the court?" he asked of Hatach.

"The prime minister is in the court, Your Majesty."

"Ah, faithful Haman! Have him proceed into the throne room.

He finished breakfast and upon entering the throne room found Haman already there. Skilled at reading the king's moods, Haman noted how fresh Ahasuerus looked, as if he had slept well and was content with the world.

"Greetings, Haman," said Ahasuerus jauntily. "I am glad you are here early."

Haman smiled. "0 King, live forever. How glowing and rested Your Majesty looks this morning! There is, if I am not mistaken, no matter of particular importance troubling my king today."

"I have only one problem, which I would like to discuss with you. Because I know that you are my only real friend, I want you to give me your advice. The question is: How may I fittingly honor a man who has rendered me a great service?"

No one would have suspected from Haman's courteous smile the thoughts that were revolving in his mind at the king's words. Self-engrossed as he was, he leapt to the conclusion that it was he whom the king meant to honor. And why not?

But he would feign aloofness, and when the king announced that the man to be honored was himself, he would pretend surprise. He would act the part of humility. He would say, "No, no, Your Majesty. It is too much!"

"Ah," he replied smoothly, "what reward is too high for the man whom my lord the king delights to honor? Would Your Majesty truly honor this man? Then give him the supreme honor! Let him ride Your Majesty's own horse, wearing your own robe of state with your gold chain about his neck, your ring upon his finger, and a royal diadem on his head. And let some high noble, one of your most intimate friends, array the man as would a menial who serves him. And let this person go before the man throughout the whole city proclaiming that whomsoever the king honors, shall be honored throughout the king's dominions."

He had said it. He had thought of everything. Now it only remained for him to put on a great show of amazement and humility.

"That is an excellent idea, Haman! Go, then, order the horse, the garment, the chain, the ring and the diadem and give them to one named Mordecai who stands in the outer court."

Haman's astonishment was not feigned. "Mordecai!"

Great as was the prime minister's consternation, he was so versed in diplomacy that he choked back the words that were on his lips. He looked into the king's radiant young face and repeated that hated name. "Mordecai?"

"Yes." Ahasuerus was beaming at him. "Let it be done this day. Make haste."

"I?"

"Yes. Fulfill all that you have spoken. Give Mordecai the things for his own—the horse, the robe, the chain, ring and diadem. Order him to dress in the garments at once and assist him to do so, for you are my most intimate friend. Too, you are the one who will go before him on foot throughout the city, proclaiming that whosoever the king honors shall be honored throughout the empire. Let it be known to Mordecai that this is his reward for preserving my life."

"Preserving Your Majesty's life? Mordecai?"

"Did you not know that it was he who warned me of the conspiracy of Bigthan and Teresh?"

"I—no, Your Majesty. I knew not the name of the man who did this."

Haman hesitated. He thought of saying that he was ill and could not do this thing. Then he remembered that if he pleaded illness, he would not be expected to go to the queen's dinner that night. He dared not refuse to obey the king's order. It was impossible now to speak to Ahasuerus about that gallows.

"Your Majesty knows that the man who saved your precious life deserves honor from me and from all. With Your Majesty's leave, I will proceed upon the matter at once."

Outside in the corridor Haman stopped and made a desperate effort to control himself. He, an Amalekite, to walk before a Hebrew! And this particular one! How could he get out of it? But there was no way. He cursed the king. He cursed the throne. He cursed the Jews. That man will sit upon a horse—above me! I will walk before him singing his praises! I will even have to help him dress!

Half an hour later a spirited black horse, caparisoned with tassels of gold, was waiting at a side entrance of the palace. In a small room immediately off this entrance was Haman. On a chair was the king's robe—purple, the color restricted to nobility. There, too, was the wide gold chain, the coveted diadem, the ring. And Mordecai was to wear them! Mordecai was to keep them for his own. Haman's hands were moist with sweat, yet his body was cold.

The door opened and Mordecai entered, astonished to see Haman there alone.

"My lord the prime minister," began Mordecai coldly, "I was sent here by a man named Hatach."

Haman spoke icily. "The king desires to honor you for saving his life. The things"— he motioned toward the chair — "as well as His Majesty's horse, are given you for your own. You are to put on the robes and ride through the city while I go before you proclaiming that whosoever the king honors must be honored throughout the realm."

Nothing could have surprised Mordecai more. He stared at Haman, thinking that this was some trick.

Haman's eyes were bright and bitter. "Take off that sackcloth," he ordered. "Do as you are told. Why do you stand staring? Let us get this thing over."

The thought came to Mordecai that this was some mockery, some plot of Haman's. "You know that I and my nation are to perish through your connivings, yet you summon me here to laugh at my calamity! You are vile and treacherous! You —"

"I am fulfilling the king's decree, a decree which, by the gods, I would rather die than obey! Yes, I hate you. I hate you more than any man on earth. I hate your race. However, my day is coming. Oh, how I will laugh—then!"

Meeting Haman's eyes squarely, Mordecai quoted from one of the ancient Hebrew psalms. *"The wicked have drawn out the sword and have set their bow to cast down the poor and needy and to slay such as are of upright conversation."*

"Put on that robe!"

Haman's intensity convinced Mordecai that this was not a hoax. Thoughtfully, he began taking off his sackcloth. The king had indeed bestowed this high honor upon him, but what did it mean? Nothing. In a few months he would be dead. He donned the purple robe, put the chain about his neck, the ring on his finger, the diadem on his head.

He looked regal and splendid, and because he wore the diadem as if it belonged to him, Haman hated him the more. He hated him so much that the words which would have given voice to this hate, choked him and he could not speak. Turning, he went out of the room, motioning Mordecai to follow.

They walked to the place where the sleek, beautiful horse pawed upon the ground with dainty, restless hoofs. Mordecai sprang upon the animal's back and Haman took the reins in his hand. Through the streets of Shushan they went, Haman leading the horse and crying out, "Behold, this is the reward your king bestows upon one who has rendered him a service—Behold, this is the man whom the king delights to honor—"

Haman's wife, his sons and his friends stood speechless at the sight. The people bowed and looked with admiring eyes upon Mordecai sitting so erect upon his horse and seemingly unmoved by the adulation. Down into the Hebrew quarter they went, and the people ceased their mourning temporarily, wondering how such a curious thing could have happened.

The whole city knew about the man whom the king delighted to honor, except Esther and her servants, who were concerned with the details of the dinner for three.

When the rounds of the city had been accomplished, Mordecai with his horse and his purple robe, his gold chain and his diadem went home, and his own people clustered about him asking what it meant.

"It means nothing," he told them. "Nothing has changed. Place your hopes in God and the queen, not in me. What you saw was but a hollow show. I have no influence with the king. Once I did him a service. He remembered me and has rewarded me. Now it is over."

Haman returned to his own house and there, confronting him in the courtyard was that gaunt, extraordinarily high gallows.

His wife put her hands on her hips and looked at him reproachfully. "Well!" she sneered. "It would seem that the day turned out slightly different from what my lord expected!"

He was tired, having walked up one street and down another in the sun. He was in no mood for talk, in no mood for the approaching dinner, but he dressed for it with care. He knew that his servants were whispering about him. He knew that the whole city was saying that the prime minister had been forced to honor the very man who had refused to bow before him.

Yes, they were smiling and shrugging in Shushan this night. Never had Haman been so disturbed. While dressing him, his servant dropped a comb. The sound startled him so that he screamed and knocked the fellow down with his fist. His wife came in.

"The sun is even now sinking. Soon the queen's servants will come for my lord. You must compose yourself."

"Get out!" he roared. "Get out of here!"

But she stood looking at him, her eyes afire with an old, old hatred which she had never before dared reveal. "If Mordecai be the seed of the Jews," she hissed, "before whom you have begun to fall, you will never prevail against him, but you will surely fall before him!"

"And whose idea was the gallows?" he sneered.

"It was mine. And how you failed in the project! The whole city laughs at you this night. 'A good joke on the prime minister,' they are saying, 'a good joke on Haman.' "

"Get out!" he screamed in maniacal fury. "Get out before I kill you!"

She looked at him—a long, insolent look. Then she left, and the room was silent again.

He had begun to fall before the Hebrews! He'd get even with her for that lie! Haman's eyeballs felt like burning coals. His head was pounding with pain from that long walk in the sun. Well, all the city would hear that on the day he walked before a Jew, he had had the honor of dining privately with the king and queen. He would see that this was publicized. But, somehow, he contemplated the coming event without elation.

In the queen's palace all was ready. Esther inspected the table, the gold wine cups, the gold plates. She breathed deeply of the sweetly scented air, gave the musicians final instructions, moved one of the lamps, gave extra thumps to the cushions of the three ornate chairs.

"The wicked watches the righteous and seeks to slay him," she muttered, quoting, as all Hebrews were apt to do, from their revered treasury of psalms. Then, smiling a little, she recalled another excerpt from the same source. *"He made a pit and digged it, and is fallen into the ditch which he has made. His mischief shall return upon his own head, and his violent dealing shall come down upon his own pate."*

She summoned the servants who were to be on duty, inspecting them to make sure their tunics were spotless, their hair freshly coiffed, their nails clean.

"Have no fear, Your Majesty," said Acratheus. "Everything is in order."

She sighed. "I would that this night were over."

Esther left the room and climbed the wide stairs. Looking after her, Acratheus wondered why she was giving this dinner. Haman, of all people, coming here! He had the feeling that something of vast importance was to happen this night.

When the sun had entirely disappeared, he called Sabuchadas and five other eunuchs. "Go to the house of the prime minister. Carry flares to light his way and escort him into the queen's presence."

Mystified, the men whispered among themselves as they walked out of the main gate. Arriving at the house of the prime minister, they stopped to stare at the gallows, looming grim and tall in the light of their flares. Then they knocked on the door and told the servant that they had come from the queen to escort the prime minister to her palace.

"My lord Haman will be down in a moment."

"So be it," answered Sabuchadas. "But tell us, what is the reason for that gallows?"

"My lord had it built last night intending to hang upon it this morning a man by the name of Mordecai. Good joke, eh?"

"Joke?"

"Yes, for this very day he went through the city crying out that the king chose to honor this man." The servant chuckled. "Well, wait here. My lord will join you presently."

The door closed. The men looked at one another in astonishment. "Mordecai!" whispered Sabuchadas. "Is not that the name of the queen's uncle, the one to whom she sends messages by Acratheus?"

"Yes, that is his name. It must be the same man, for it is not a name much heard in Shushan."

"So," mused Sabuchadas, "Haman would hang the queen's uncle! Now, here is a curious thing. Haman builds a gallows for the queen's uncle, and this very night the queen invites Haman to dine with her and the king. Hmm. That gallows is at least fifty cubits high. Haman surely meant that all the city should see Mordecai hanging. Now, by the gods, I am glad I am to be on duty in the banquet hall this night! I have a feeling that something is going to happen which I would not want to miss!"

13: The Green Bay Tree

HIS MAJESTY was satisfied with life. He had preserved the peace of his country. The harvests had been plentiful. He had that day instituted provision for the digging of more public wells. He had planned a hunting trip into the rugged mountains. He had had an excellent dinner. He had enjoyed the soothing music. His good friend Haman had been fascinating and witty throughout the meal.

The handsome young monarch leaned back in his chair. It was good, just to relax like this with the two people he loved most in the world. Such an occasion was something of an event in his harried, hard-working existence.

He looked across the table at his wife, slim, girlish, utterly lovely in that gown of deep purple. Stationed near by were his bodyguards. Behind the chairs, experts at serving, stood Acratheus and Sabuchadas. Trusted servitors these, and Ahasuerus thought of the gifts he would give them before leaving. Indeed, he felt in so generous a mood that tonight he loved all the world and feared no one.

"And now, Esther, yesterday you said you had a petition to ask of me. Tell me the gift you desire. Be assured that in all the world whatever you wish you shall have."

Haman smiled and nodded. "A queen so beautiful, so chaste and so charming should have no unfulfilled wish. To the Persians, Esther has become more goddess than queen. They worship her everywhere, and tonight my own nearness to her presence adds to my enchantment. Lovely, lovely is Persia's queen; noble, just and wise is her king."

His voice was low and caressing. His eyes, turning from the king to rest upon Esther, were bold. No longer could she endure those eyes and their surreptitious, ogling glances. Her face grew suddenly tense. She called out nervously, "Let the music cease. Let the musicians depart."

Abruptly, in the midst of a strain, the melody broke off. Without it the big room seemed strangely still; an unbroken stillness, stretching on and on, in its vastness seeming to encompass the world. Watching his wife, Ahasuerus saw her face grow pale.

"My love," he murmured softly, "surely you can speak to me without fear. What is your petition? It shall be granted, even to the half of my kingdom."

"My lord the king, now I recall there is a saying of my people, *The righteousness of the upright shall deliver them, but the transgressors shall be taken in their own naughtiness.*"

What was she afraid of? Why was she trembling so? Was she afraid to put her husband to the test? Was she afraid that he would justify the slaughter or make excuses for Haman?

Haman nodded. "I know not where this quotation comes from, but it is a sage one."

With an effort, Esther controlled herself, and went on as though he had not spoken. "If I have found favor in your sight,

O King, and if it please the king, let my *life* be given at my petition and that of my people be given at my request!"

"Your—life?" queried Ahasuerus.

"Your Majesty's people?" asked Haman.

"Yes," went on Esther, excitedly now. "We are to be destroyed, to perish!"

"How? When? What do you mean?" asked her husband.

"Your Majesty knows that a decree has gone forth from the throne room that every member of my nation shall be slain."

"Your nation?" asked the king.

"Your nation?" echoed Haman. "Your Majesty is a—"

"I am—a Hebrew!" Across the expanse of table their eyes met. Hers did not waver.

Haman knew why she had invited him now. Inwardly, he groaned. She wanted him, an Amalekite, to plead with the king to spare the Jews, to add his influence to hers! He wondered how he could make a quick exit. Apprehensively he glanced over his shoulder to ascertain how far he was from the door. His hands were like ice. He reached for the wine cup, but his grasp shook so that he spilled some of its contents on the cloth.

Esther's face was firm. There was no quivering now, no compromise, no hesitation. "My lord," she continued, eyes imploringly upon the king, "life is good. It is likewise good to those women in the Hebrew quarter. I make this petition, not for myself, but for them. Spare them. Oh, spare them!"

"Women? I made no decree against women, but against traitors, against troublemakers, rebels."

"Indeed, my lord, you made it against women, against little children. I would not have troubled you in this matter if the decree had been that they were to be sold as slaves. If they had been sold as bondmen and bondwomen I would have held my tongue, but now I desire that they might be delivered from death—men, women, young girls, infants, old people! And I am among those who will die, yet it is not for myself that I plead, but for those others! Oh, I cannot believe that you are the author of this misery! No. You know the man who is the cause of it!"

"I? Know him? Where is he? Who dared presume to do a thing like this?"

"The adversary," said Esther, "is this wicked Haman!"

Stunned, incredulous, the king looked from one face to the other, unable to speak.

What is she talking about, he asked himself wildly. How could a thing like this be? Could I have been such a fool? How can she accuse good old Haman? Has she brought my friend here, not to honor him, but to insult him?

For once in his life, Haman was at a loss for words. "Her Majesty has been misinformed."

Esther was master of the situation now. She rose, white and regal, pointing the finger of accusation at him. "You are evil, Haman, evil to the core of you, rotten with hatred, puffed up like a toad with your lust for power!"

"No, my queen, no. I swear I am a patriotic Persian, loving my king and country more than my life!"

"You love nothing on earth but yourself. You are concerned only with your own self-interest." From her wide belt she took the decree and held it toward her husband. "Here is the proof! To this atrocious document Your Majesty's seal is set. You will notice that we are not given the right to lift one hand in our own defense. We are ordered to submit—to death! And how was the date of this massacre set? By the casting of lots!"

Haman blanched. He had not intended that Ahasuerus would ever see that document. "My queen!" he begged wildly. "If I have offended you, I ask your forgiveness. See, on my knees I ask it! I swear I have not done wrong, and if I have, I had the king's permission. He gave me his ring to put his seal on the paper. I did only—"

"You have lied to him about my people! Produce, if you can, one instance wherein the Hebrews have stirred up trouble in the land or refused to obey the laws! These people have harmed no one. They ask only to bring up their children and live in peace. They are grateful to His Majesty for the freedom they have enjoyed. For years, Haman, ever since you came to power, the Amalekites have beaten them, cheated them, and they have had no redress in the courts."

To Ahasuerus, the scene taking place before him had all the aspects of the impossible. Esther's fiery denunciation had come so suddenly and unexpectedly that he was confused by it. His hitherto gentle wife was now possessed of dynamic force and mastery. His once suave and genial Haman was actually cowering.

"Her Majesty knows," Haman was saying humbly, "that I am only a human being. We humans are not infallible. I may have made a terrible mistake. I admit I did advise His Majesty in this matter, but the affair had the full agreement of the councillors. They unanimously agreed to it. They are then as much to blame as I."

"The councillors!" Esther turned her glowing eyes upon her husband. "Look back, Your Majesty. Think! Have any of them ever disagreed with anything this—this creature has said? They are afraid of him! He has corrupted them all. I beg my lord to consider what would have happened had I not invited you here and confronted you with this barbarous decree which otherwise you might never have seen. When the day of the massacre was over, your esteemed Haman would have met you with smiles and told you that the thing had been accomplished. You would have mutually congratulated each other. If by chance it reached your ears that babies and women had been slain, Haman would have shrugged, saying that it was inevitable that a few foolish women had somehow thrust themselves in the way of the Amalekite swords. But in his plotting, he had not figured that I, your wife, would have taken my place among my people and that one of those swords would have found my heart!"

Ahasuerus read the decree swiftly, horrified at its brutality. Certain phrases stood out mockingly. "Haman, prudent and just—motivated by his fidelity toward me—the Amalekites are—to cause to perish Jews both young and old, little children, infants and women—"

With an ejaculation of disgust, he crumpled it in his big hand. "You have said to me, Haman, that these people were traitors and troublemakers, that they were engaged in fomenting a rebellion. I had fallen into the habit of taking your word without question, because I trusted you. Now then, give me proof, tangible proof, of your statements."

"I—I—" Haman clutched the back of the chair, leaning heavily upon it. "I have no actual proof, but—but I have heard—"

"You lied, then, when you said there was danger of a rebellion."

"Yes," admitted Haman, desperately now, "I lied. I crave forgiveness. I beg Your Majesty to—"

"Why did you lie?"

"Because I"—the small eyes glittered with savagery—"I hate the Hebrews!"

He knew now that any defense he might make would be futile. During the long silence which followed, his black eyes darted anxiously from one face to the other. He kept asking himself what he could say in his own defense. He groped for words with which to plead his own case. But none came.

"And how many other times must you have lied to me during these years!" said Ahasuerus in a tone of sorrow mingled with amazement. "And how many times have I comforted myself when burdens and problems seemed more than I could bear, with the thought that I could always rely upon good old Haman! What is so despicable as a man who abuses another's trust?"

Like all Persians, Ahasuerus considered lying one of the most hideous of sins. Haman thought of that, now, knowing that the king was thinking of it. In terror he asked himself why he had been such a fool as to confess to being a liar. What can I say? he thought. What can I say?

But he who had always been so glib, could think of nothing except the roaring of the blood in his head and the furious pounding of his heart. If he could only somehow quiet his heart, then he could think, then he could speak words of appeasement.

"I—I have always cherished my lord the king—" he mumbled thickly.

"Liar! Liar!" cried Ahasuerus.

He sat, deeply moved, thinking back, realizing that the councillors did always agree with Haman. Other things came clearly to mind. Bigthan and Teresh accusing this man of being the instigator of the plot. They had spoken the truth! The engineer whom Haman had so highly recommended, into whose hands had been entrusted the costly project of the sea wall! Remembering these things now made Ahasuerus physically sick. How blind he had been!

Ahasuerus the mighty! What a mockery it was!

His "good old Haman" was malicious, cruel, and must have despised him all along. Shocked and pained, the king was as a man who receives a sudden and deadly wound. He was suffering acutely, but he must forget his pain, his self-reproaches, his disillusionment, to consider the magnitude of this shameful decree. Innocent people to be slaughtered, even infants! And his own wife one of the doomed—Esther, his beloved!

Guilt was clearly written on the dark face of the prime minister. He began pleading, his voice assuming a disagreeable whine, his malignant eyes glittering with panic.

"Mercy, Queen Esther!"

"Do you expect pity, you who are pitiless?" she cried.

"Yes, for you are merciful, you are gracious, you are kind. I beg you to forgive me. Forgive! Plead for me with my lord, the valiant king! Had I known, would I—would I—no, no! I am old. Spare my life. I confess I have done wrong. But now I am shattered. I—am beaten. Have pity!"

From behind the queen's chair, Sabuchadas burst out impulsively. "I crave leave to speak!" Before receiving permission to do so, he went on. "If His Majesty will go to Haman's house he will find in his courtyard a gallows fifty cubits tall. It was erected last night, prepared for a man named Mordecai, constructed because Mordecai refused to bow down to him!"

"Mordecai!" exclaimed Ahasuerus. "The one who saved my life! The man whom I honored only today. And you would hang this man because he did not bow down to you? Are you a god, then, that you must be worshipped?"

"Your Majesty," whimpered Haman, "have mercy on me!"

"I have known this man Mordecai for years," spoke up Acratheus, "and never have I heard him speak anything but praise for the king."

"Pity," sobbed Haman, "pity!"

"You showed no pity for others." The king turned to Sabuchadas. "Find this Mordecai. Bring him here."

"Mordecai is my uncle," said Esther, as Sabuchadas left.

"Your uncle?" gasped Haman. He moaned and fell at the queen's feet, groveling, hysterical.

"Enough of this," cried Ahasuerus. "You plotted my life as well. You did not know when you built that gallows that you were building it for yourself. What you have devised for others, you yourself shall receive."

"No, no, not that! In mercy's name, spare me! Spare me!"

"Take him away," commanded Ahasuerus to his axemen. "Take him away and hang him immediately upon the gallows he has built."

Sobbing, pleading, Haman was led out of the house.

"Justice has been done," said Ahasuerus. "I give his estate to you, Esther."

"To me? But what good will it do me? Think you I would live to watch all my people die?" Now sobbing unrestrainedly, she fell at his feet. "If it please the king, if I have found favor in his eyes, and if the thing seem right to the king, let the *reverse* of the letter by Haman be written! Reverse that letter which he wrote to destroy every Hebrew in the king's provinces!"

"Rise, Esther, my love; don't sob so. I—I cannot reverse it! I—cannot revoke it!"

"But how can I endure to see this evil come upon my people? How can I endure to see the destruction of my own kindred?"

The king gave her a long, dazed look. Then he turned and went out into the private court. It seemed to him that there was fever in the night itself. He thought of Haman and his subtle speeches, and he was filled with disgust. Back and forth Ahasuerus paced, not caring whether or not he kept to the path. Depressed, angry, he raged against himself, telling himself what a fool he had been. He was amazed at the things which had been going on all around him for years, things which he had not known, he who was an absolute monarch!

Sounds came from the house—the clink of cutlery, some maids washing the supper dishes, humming, murmuring, laughing. The musicians, eating in the servants' dining room, and getting drunk.

"They didn't like our music," bellowed a sullen voice. "They sent us away early. We should have played something gayer for the king. He likes gay music."

Ahasuerus shuddered and turned back to another part of the court. Gay music! Would there ever be gaiety in his heart again? He had thought of all people in the world he could always trust Haman. But why did his mind keep reverting to Haman? It was this decree he must consider now. His Esther had petitioned him to save her people. Esther. Mordecai, the man who had saved his life; yet now, when Mordecai's life was in danger, he, the king, was powerless to save it!

Esther, one of the doomed. How could he look into her clear eyes again? How could he tell her that he was helpless? Yes, helpless. He wanted above all things to make her happy—and had he brought her to Shushan only to die?

Presently he heard the sound of footsteps and a knocking upon the palace door. It must be Mordecai. He must see this man.

As Mordecai entered the banquet hall by the door, the king entered it by one of the long windows in the garden. Mordecai had put on the purple robe and fine linen, and he wore the diadem of gold.

Recognizing the king, he knelt. "O King, live forever."

"Rise, Mordecai," said Ahasuerus.

Esther, who had obviously been crying, came and stood by her uncle's side, although they did not touch each other.

As Mordecai rose, the two tall men looked long and deeply into each other's eyes. Gazing out from Mordecai's strong face were the same clear, honest eyes of Esther. Studying Mordecai's face, Ahasuerus noted the firm chin, the straight, though prominent nose. This man, thought Ahasuerus, is wise. He will not always agree with me because I wear the crown. And that is good. I am sick of being toadied to. I am sick of smoothness and guile.

"I sent for you, Mordecai, to see what manner of man you are. This night I have learned that you are my wife's uncle. You have my leave to visit her when you wish. Take this ring. It is a ring of state. It will give you entry to the queen's palace and to mine."

"Your Majesty has already done much for me this day, but the permission to visit my niece means even more to me."

"And this, also, may mean something more to you—your enemy, Haman, is dead."

"Dead! As it is written, *I have seen the wicked in great power, and spreading himself like a green bay tree—yet he passed away, and lo, he was not.*"

"The green bay tree has, indeed, passed away," said Ahasuerus. "I have no prime minister. I now offer that post to you."

"I thank Your Majesty and I vow to serve you to the best of my ability, but—" A twisted smile played about Mordecai's mouth. "Your Majesty knows that this service will not be for long."

"Uncle Mordecai," said Esther, "the king has given me Haman's estate. I now turn it over to you."

"It is a vast and wealthy estate," said Mordecai gravely. "Wealth gotten through graft. I will take it and distribute as much as possible to the poor. I am a plain man, Your Majesty. I want little. A few months only I shall live in that house, unless—"

"O Ahasuerus," begged Esther, all formality forgotten, "my lord, my love, deliver my people from death! You have only to speak the word. If my people are destroyed, I could not bear to live! If you love me, avert this massacre!"

"I would do anything to avert it, but I cannot!"

"Cannot? *You*—cannot?"

"Does the king say," asked Mordecai unbelievingly, "that there is something he cannot do?"

"There is but one thing I can do. Acratheus, send for the scribes." Ahasuerus sat down, his eyes upon Mordecai. "I cannot revoke my former decree for the slaughter of your people. What is sealed with the king's ring, no man can reverse."

"Not even the king?" asked Esther.

"Not even I."

"Your Majesty," stated Mordecai, "the decree as written commands our annihilation. We could not, therefore, even attempt to protect ourselves. If, then, you cannot revoke this mandate, then, in God's name, at least give us leave to defend ourselves!"

The king nodded. "That is my intention, but this is all I can do. I can send a letter to the governors of each province. Oh, I am wretched, wretched, filled with remorse and grief that this should have happened!"

"But the letter?" asked Esther in a choked voice.

"All I can do in this letter is to empower the Hebrews to fight. Fight for their lives! Let it be a fight between Amalekite and Hebrew, and all outsiders excluded. If any person, any Amalekite, attempt to destroy them—let the Hebrews fight! Every desert animal has the right of self-defense. Listen, both of you. The Medes and the Persians have an old law. I have meant to abolish this law, but I have not yet done so, and now I cannot for one year, for there is a time set for such changes. The law is that whatever decree is signed by the king and his councillors is changeless. This document has nine seals. The seals of all were put to it that day. Thus a royal statute is established. It cannot be broken."

"So be it," said Mordecai. "But at least we need not submit to death meekly. We can arm ourselves and be ready. If we are permitted to fight, then fight we shall!"

"How many Amalekites are in the kingdom?" asked Esther.

"Seventy-five thousand eight hundred by the last census," replied Ahasuerus.

"I recall a prophecy by a man named Balaam, said Mordecai. *"Amalek was the first of the nations, but his later end shall be that he perish forever."*

He walked to his niece. "Hadassah, my dear child!" He kissed her on the brow.

How good it was to hear the old childish name again! Esther was finding now some measure of serenity. She even smiled at her uncle, the submissive, tender smile of the old days in Babylon.

The scribes entered and placed their small tables on the floor in front of the king. Out of their bundles of sharpened pens each scribe selected one, holding it in position.

No longer was Ahasuerus shaken. He was a man of vigor as he began dictating one of the most important letters in the history of the Hebrews.

14: Purim

ESTHER, eyes fixed upon her husband, sank upon a divan. Mordecai sat beside her, both of them rigid with suspense. Her hand crept into his and he held it firmly, as though she were not a queen but a little, frightened child.

The big room was empty except for the scribes and the three members of the royal family. The king sat, his well-shaped head lowered, his eyes upon a space of wall.

"The great King Ahasuerus to our rulers and our loyal subjects, greeting.

"There are men who, because of the enormity of the benefits we have bestowed upon them and because of our kind treatment which has given them exalted positions and honors, have proven injurious to their inferiors. Such natures do not even scruple to do evil to their benefactors.

"Such men, having no gratitude, insolently abuse the benefits conferred upon them and turn against those who are the source of their abundance. As their guile succeeds, these men have the effrontery to believe that they can hide from God and avoid the punishment which in justice comes from Him.

"One such man, deceiving those in power, persuaded them to be angered against those who had done them no harm, until now these people are in danger of perishing."

He looked across the room into Esther's eyes, saw the shudder that went through that slender, graceful body. She nodded, urging him on. He continued.

"This deception has brought forth a deplorable result, and now, in the matter of rectification, we have no ancient examples to guide us.

"This day we learned that it is no longer possible to pay any attention to such calumnies. From now on we will seek out proof and determine for ourselves what has been done, and having this knowledge, punish only those who are guilty. Such has been the case with Haman, son of Hammed-atha, by birth an Amalekite. This man partook of that kindness, which we bear to all men, in so great a degree as to be called father.

"However, he did not govern honestly the magnitude of his position. We gave him authority, and against us who had given him authority, he made a conspiracy.

"Also, he endeavored to hang Mordecai, our benefactor and the uncle of Esther, partner of our life and our dominion. We now perceive that this pernicious fellow had set his mind to the destruction of the Hebrews, not because they are disloyal to the government, but because of a personal animosity to them.

"We, therefore, by this epistle, free them from the punishment decreed in our former letter—the letter that was prompted and sent by Haman; consequently, if you refuse obedience to it, you will do well.

"In Shushan we have hanged the man who contrived the destruction of the Hebrews.

"We charge you to make public copy of this epistle throughout our kingdom, that the Hebrews may be permitted peaceably to pursue their business and religion.

"We further decree that on the day formerly specified for their destruction, they may defend themselves from violence.

"It is our belief that God has made that day a day of salvation to them instead of destruction.

"Take notice that every city, every province, that shall disobey anything contained herein shall be destroyed by fire. Let this epistle be published throughout the country.

"Let the Hebrews be ready for the day afore mentioned, that they may be avenged of their enemies.

"To this we set our seal."

A scribe held out a box of black wax. The king removed his ring of office, dipped it into the box, and pressed it to the bottom of the document. Then he addressed the chief scribe.

"See that this is sent at once by every means—horses, mules, donkeys, camels. That is all. I shall not want any of you any more tonight." When the scribes had gone, he turned to Esther and her uncle. "I can do no more," he murmured helplessly.

"All we ask is a fair chance to defend ourselves," replied Mordecai. "When the specified day comes, we shall be ready. I am glad now that it is some moons away, for we have few weapons among us and the smiths will have time to make them."

"And will you win?" asked Ahasuerus.

"I cannot predict future events, Your Majesty. I know that in the days of my ancestor, Saul, we met the Amalekites and defeated them. Not that they were cowards. They fought bravely. Nevertheless, we vanquished them. We fought them in the towns and in the wilderness, and we shall do so again."

"But in those days," said Esther, "we had an army of trained warriors. Now we have no trained warriors."

Neither man answered.

After a slight pause, Mordecai rose. "I must not keep Your Majesties. Have I your permission to leave?"

Ahasuerus held out his hand to him. "Tomorrow you will take your rightful place in my household. Let us be forever at peace with one another."

"As my king has said. Let us be forever at peace."

Mordecai spoke calmly. Indeed, a deep calmness had settled in the room. Through that calmness the two men estimated each other. Then with a bow to Esther and the king, Mordecai went out. Now, as though swept toward him by a mighty breeze, Esther was in the king's arms.

"Oh, hold me close to you!" she whispered.

"My love! Do you realize how great is the service you have given this night to me and to your people? I think they will never forget that you, a girl, have saved them from destruction."

"They are not yet saved."

"Perchance some will die upon that day, but many will live to bless the name of Esther," he prophesied.

In every Hebrew household now there was a speedy accumulation of arms. At once old men, middle-aged men and boys began training in the use of the lance and the spear.

The Amalekites, now that they knew they would have to fight rather than merely slaughter, spent hours practicing with their weapons. Remembering too vividly their ancient shame, they faced the day with dread.

Outsiders decided upon a policy of non-interference. This thing was solely betwixt Hebrew and Amalekite. Others would keep off the streets and barricade their houses upon that gory day.

As weeks passed, seemingly with willful slowness, the strain increased. Finally came the morning for which everyone had waited. Shops were closed. Houses were shuttered. Even the outer court of the king was empty.

At daybreak Ahasuerus came to the house of the queen. "How is it with my Esther?"

"It is well."

"I hold no audiences today. I have ordered men stationed throughout the land to bring us reports as quickly as possible."

Scarcely had he spoken than cries of agony began to reach them from the city. The fighting had begun. Esther ran to a window and looked down upon the streets.

Hour after hour messengers covered with sweat arrived at the queen's palace with reports. From the window Esther saw men fighting, sometimes in crowds, sometimes a pair of them hand to hand. From this distance it was impossible to distinguish Jew from Amalekite. As moments passed and the screams did not abate, her face grew wan and her eyes glittered with anxiety.

Noon came. She and her husband sat opposite each other at table, but neither could eat.

Beneath a sky that was clear and tranquil, turmoil reigned. It seemed to Esther that the day would never end. The world was a universe of pain, pain that throbbed, pain that tore through space like a cyclone.

What side was winning? Reports varied.

"The Amalekites are winning in Parmasta!" exclaimed Ahasuerus; and two hours later, "The Hebrews are winning in Arisai!"

The sun sank, and with its sinking every street was lit by torches. The red glow seemed to reach even to the starlit sky.

The tumult of the conflict, instead of subsiding, had intensified. If the nightingales were still singing, it was impossible to hear them. Servants brought in lights, moving on tiptoe, as though they dreaded to add another sound to the uproar. They lit the braziers as if in the hope that the sweet smell of the incense would help to make things normal again.

"Another report, Your Majesty," cried Sabuchadas. "The fight goes evenly, neither side winning, in Vajezatha!"

Esther shuddered. "Man killing man! It sickens me. I hate it. I hate it!"

"Would you have me put an end to it?" asked Ahasuerus.

"No! We must continue—until we conquer!"

The dark dragged on, seemingly into eternity. But with the approach of dawn the city began to grow quiet. The streets were slippery with blood. Weary fighters stumbled over bodies; some of these lay still in death, others were moaning in agony, writhing, shrieking.

The king summoned Acratheus and Sabuchadas. "Find Mordecai. If he is still alive, see if you can do him any service. If he is able, tell him to come here at once."

While it was still dark, Hatach arrived. "This is the last report from Shushan and the immediate vicinity, Your Majesty."

Ahasuerus took it eagerly, and began rapidly adding the totals of the many reports which had been delivered throughout the night.

Her face drawn and pallid, Esther watched him tensely.

"Well?" she asked at last.

"Well, at least in Shushan, your people are victors. Five hundred Amalekites have been killed in the city. We don't yet know for certain the results in the provinces."

"Five hundred," she repeated thoughtfully.

He spoke gently but with intense earnestness. "Esther, on this occasion, *you* are the general in command. You must make the decision. Do you wish the fighting to continue another day or will you end it—now?"

Her big eyes took on a wild, startled expression. Her whole body pulsed with dread. Hers the decision! Hers the responsibility! More bloodshed. No! No! All day it had seemed that the flashing lances had pierced through her own flesh, again, again and again! She, as much as those fighters in the streets, had quivered with pain, reeled in torment. No more of it. Let it end. Let it be forgotten like some horrible nightmare.

And yet—and yet—oh, steady, now. What was the *right* thing, what was the wise thing to do? Oh, think clearly. Consider. Remnants of a deadly and unscrupulous force remained. As months passed, those remnants, sly and unprincipled, would gather strength. Bitter, brooding, they would wait for another time to arise as a threat to peace. She saw now for the first time that this was bigger than the mere problem of Jew versus Amalekite. The Amalekites stood for an aggressive, greedy, bullying force—a force which, if not stopped, would expand and threaten the security of *all* peace-loving men.

"O dear God," she mumbled aloud, "help me to do *Thy* will!"

The words, frantically uttered, brought steadiness. God was good. Good. Good. If God was good, then surely it was His will that evil be utterly destroyed. If God was good, then surely—oh, surely, He would not tolerate an evil power to menace the well-being of those who believed in Him!

She had completely forgotten her husband, whose eyes were fixed upon her steadily—eyes that understood the intensity of her suffering, eyes charged with pity for her in this dreadful moment.

But he said nothing. He waited. And witnessing the ghastly pallor of that young face, he thought he *knew* what her decision would be.

For twenty-four hours he had observed her. He had seen how she winced at every cry of pain. He had seen how acutely she had suffered. Now, that pallid face, the trembling of those little hands testified to the fact that she was on the verge of collapse. After all, she was a woman, and women were weak creatures, tenderhearted and shortsighted in such matters. So he fully expected her to cry out: "No! No! It is enough! I cannot endure any more of this!"

But he was a warrior and he was a statesman. He knew that peace was not to be bought so cheaply. He knew that, in the end, a mere partial victory was costly and foolish. It gave the enemy a chance to fight again in the future. It enabled the enemy to boast of being unvanquished. And so long as an enemy could do that, he remained a potential threat. But one could scarcely expect a woman to have this knowledge. One could scarcely expect a woman to have the courage to keep fighting, especially when it was so much easier at this point to accept an incomplete victory.

Having reasoned in this manner, Ahasuerus was astounded when, after a seemingly interminable silence, Esther's voice rang out decisively.

"No! We haven't yet won this battle! The enemy is not thoroughly beaten! Only when victory is complete can we be assured of peace and security!"

He gazed at her, appalled, but speechless with admiration. Gentle though she was, she was no weakling. Here was wisdom, here was courage, here was stamina!

"So be it," he said, in a tone of deep respect.

Swiftly, he dictated messages to the scribes. Swiftly, the *angari* carried them to the authorities of Shushan and to every place round about that could be reached in time.

It was dawn when Mordecai entered the palace. His face was dirty, his clothes were torn and soaked with sweat, his usually well-groomed hair was disordered. He was utterly exhausted. The king rushed to him and embraced him.

"Thank heaven you are still alive!"

Esther came to him and clung to his arm. "You have not been hurt?"

"No. I apologize for coming before Your Majesties in this disarray, but your servant said I was to come at once. I report to the king that before the fighting began we Hebrews held a conference. As prime minister I made bold to send the decision to all other Hebrews in your dominions—that the riches of the Amalekites revert to Your Majesty's treasury . We touch none of them!"

"I honor you for that decision. And now, it is Esther's will that since there is only a partial victory, the fighting will continue."

Mordecai nodded.

Even as he did so, renewed shrieks of suffering were heard. Mordecai bowed to the king and hurried away.

"God guard him!" muttered Esther.

Next day the Hebrews proclaimed total victory. They proclaimed it with songs and dances. They held festival throughout the country. Some of them were wounded, but their casualties had been few.

Speedily the marks of conflict were erased. Outsiders removed the barricades from their windows, and told one another that eight hundred Amalekites had been slain in

Shushan, and that reports from other places read that graves had been dug for over seventy-five thousand of them.

It seemed that day that death had no longer a foothold upon the earth, and that the whole universe teemed with life. The birds sang with boldness and vitality. People became aware of spring flowers gaily blooming, of a kindly sun, revealing a newness and a freshness that they had never noticed before. And they were grateful for these things, grateful for quiet, normal things, like shops opening and people walking freely along the streets, grateful for life itself, for maidens laughing, for children playing.

In the Hebrew quarter of Shushan there was feasting, and people would leave their own feast to carry some part of it to their neighbors. They wore their best clothes. The young girls danced and the young men sang, lifting their voices lustily and exultantly. Their world was suddenly benign and good—good.

At the head of a large banquet table sat Mordecai, an illustrious person now, a man of power in the government. He rose from his place and stood looking at them, self-controlled, fatherly.

"Quiet, now," spoke up a rabbi. "The Lord Mordecai would speak to us."

"These," he began after an impressive silence, "are the days of Purim. Purim! Which, being translated, means 'lots.' But to us, henceforth and forever, the word will mean 'The Days of our Deliverance.' Each year let the Hebrews feast upon the fourteenth and fifteenth days of Adar, holding festival, giving gifts to the poor, and in love and gratitude sending portions to one another. These are the days wherein we find rest from our enemies. For us, this is the month that has turned sorrow to joy. Let us keep these days forever as days of feasting and gladness, and let us deliver these days to our posterity, that these celebrations might continue for all time. Let Purim be an interval in which to honor our great Queen Esther, a time in which we thank Almighty God for His deliverance and protection. And on these days let every Hebrew seek peace in his own heart. Let us upon these days light candles as a token of our rejoicing. As for Haman—"

"Let his name be blotted out!" cried a man.

"Let the name of the ungodly perish!" shouted another.

"Peace," went on Mordecai, as though they had not spoken. "Let Purim be a time of peace to us, wherein hatred is abolished and our hearts glow and soften with peace in ourselves and peace with our neighbors!"

And up on the hilltop, in the courtyard of the queen, Esther leaned lovingly against her husband's shoulder while he held her close. The air about them was perfumed with Arabian frankincense, mingling with the scent of countless flowers.

"Your people, my beloved," said Ahasuerus softly, "will always remember you. Never will the name of Esther be forgotten."

She smiled faintly, feeling secure and blissful within his arms. "What I have done has been for love of them. If what my lord says be so, let my name mean to them the two most precious things in all the world, peace and love. And may the peace and love which I feel this day revive like a holy benediction in their hearts each year, and may they proclaim peace and justice—to *all*!"

Publishing Note

Behold Your Queen! A Story of Esther was first published in 1951 under the title “Behold Your Queen!”.

The cover image is adapted from a painting by Ernest Normand.

For more information on Gladys Malvern books, please visit:
http://www.specialeditionbooks.com
http://www.shouston.com/gladys_malvern.html

Special Edition Books would like to thank Susan Houston for her vision, persistence and tireless work in bringing these classic books by Gladys Malvern back into print after more than 20 years of being unavailable to young people.

Printed by Amazon Italia Logistica S.r.l.
Torrazza Piemonte (TO), Italy